A CLEVER ALLIANCE: A REGENCY ROMANCE

LAURA BEERS

A Clever Alliance:
A Regency Romance

By: Laura Beers

Cover art by Blue Water Books

Created with Vellum

MORE ROMANCE FROM LAURA BEERS

The Beckett Files

Regency Spy Romances

Saving Shadow

A Peculiar Courtship

To Love a Spy

A Tangled Ruse

A Deceptive Bargain

The Baron's Daughter

Coming Soon- *The Unfortunate Debutante*

1

BATH, ENGLAND, 1812

Lady Madalene Ramsbury gripped the branches so tightly that her knuckles turned white as her toes searched for footholds on the white pine tree.

"Climbing in a dress is nearly impossible," her dear friend, Lady Isabella Beauchamp, said in a huff from below her.

Ignoring the sweat trickling down her back, she suggested, "Perhaps we should buy trousers next time we go into Town?"

Isabella laughed lightly. "Oh dear, wouldn't that be scandalous?"

Finding her usual spot to rest, Madalene pulled herself up and leaned her back against the thick tree trunk. She wiped the sweat from her forehead with the back of her hand. It was rather difficult to climb a tree, but it was worth the effort. From her vantage point, she could see the rolling green hills of Bath with cattle grazing in the distance. The blue sky seemed to sparkle in the sunlight, and on the breeze, she could hear the cheerful twitter of birds.

"You need to pick a new pastime, Maddie," Isabella teased as she leaned against a low branch. "Climbing trees is hardly appropriate for a lady."

"Neither is riding astride," Madalene bantered.

Isabella shrugged unrepentantly. "It's much easier to ride astride than with a side saddle."

Rather than argue with her friend's misguided logic, Madalene joked, "Aren't we rebels?"

"I daresay that we will need to be on our best behavior when we go to London for the Season next year."

Turning towards her blonde-haired friend, Madalene asked, "Do you regret not going home for the Season this year?"

"I do not. I am not even eighteen yet." Isabella paused. "Do you regret it?"

Madalene shook her head. "I would much rather stay at Miss Bell's Finishing School than face my horrid uncle."

"Perhaps my mother would be willing to host you for the next Season," Isabella remarked.

"Wouldn't that be grand?" Madalene murmured, growing pensive. If only her mother was still alive to prepare her for the Season. She ran her hand along her black skirt.

A long, comfortable silence descended over them, interrupted only by the sound of the birds chirping in the trees.

"Do you miss your mother?" Isabella asked.

Madalene closed her eyes. "Every single day."

"I lost my father seven years ago, but I couldn't imagine the pain of losing my mother," Isabella admitted.

"Losing my parents so close together was the hardest thing I have ever faced," Madalene replied, blinking back her tears. "I couldn't even say goodbye to them because typhoid fever is so contagious."

"I'm glad that you came back to Miss Bell's Finishing School."

Madalene huffed. "That was an easy decision. It was either that or stay with my uncle."

"Is he truly that awful?"

Pressing her lips together, Madalene admitted, "I often heard my parents discussing my uncle's gambling habits. He would frequent the gambling halls in London and spend money that he did not have."

"Was he cruel to you?"

"No, but growing up, he hardly spoke to me," she shared.

The church bell chimed in the distance, alerting them to the time.

"We better hurry back before Miss Bell discovers we're gone," Isabella said as she started climbing down.

Grabbing hold of the branch, Madalene found a foothold and quickly scampered down the tree.

"That's not fair," Isabella claimed as she finally came to stand next to her friend. "You have an uncanny ability to climb trees."

Looping arms, they started heading towards the estate. Madalene glanced at Isabella with a mischievous expression. "I'm excited to practice whitework embroidery today."

Isabella groaned. "I hate sitting around all day, working on embroidery. I would prefer to be riding on a beautiful day like this."

"You would *always* prefer to be riding."

"Yes, but I truly abhor needlework."

Madalene laughed. "But an accomplished woman must be proficient at needlework."

"Don't you ever wish that gentlemen would be interested in our *actual* thoughts and opinions rather than our abilities to play instruments and speak in demure tones?"

"I'm afraid gentlemen like that don't exist," Madalene replied as they stepped onto the cobblestone footpath leading to the main entrance of the estate.

"I overheard Penelope, Adelaide, Jo, and Caroline discussing marriage. They all decided that they would only marry for love."

"I heard them mention that, as well."

Isabella stopped and turned to face her. "Should we make the same pact?"

Madalene wanted to say yes, but something held her back. "I don't know what the future holds for me," she admitted reluctantly.

"All the more reason to only marry for love," Isabella pressed.

"What of you?"

Isabella laughed. "I'm more than happy to make the pact, but I have no intention of marrying at all."

"Why, exactly?"

Her friend tilted her pointed chin, determination in her eyes. "I refuse to marry someone that won't let me be myself... quirks and all."

"I daresay you shall have men lined up to court you."

"I think not. What gentleman would be interested in a bluestocking that enjoys riding astride?" Isabella challenged.

Madalene shook her head at her friend's tone. Isabella was a beauty with her blonde curls, fair skin, and bright, expressive eyes. She had always felt that she paled in comparison to her.

"*If* I marry," Madalene started slowly, "I will only marry for love, as well."

"That wasn't so hard, was it?" Isabella asked, grinning.

A black coach approached the estate, and Madalene saw her familial crest on the door. A feeling of dread washed over her.

"That's my uncle's coach," she shared.

Isabella turned to watch the coach as it rolled along the cobblestone street. She placed her hand above her eyes, shielding them from the sun. "Why did your uncle travel from London to call upon you?"

"I don't know, but I don't have a good feeling about it."

"You did turn eighteen last week. Perhaps he intends to present you for the Season."

"I doubt that."

Isabella grew serious, and she met her gaze. "Whatever happens, just know that you can always seek out my brother, Lord Northampton, or my mother. They're both in Town for the Season, and they will help you. I'm sure of it."

The coach jerked to a stop in front of Miss Bell's Finishing School, and a footman jumped down from the seat next to the driver. He stepped quickly to the door and knocked.

Isabella let out a sigh of relief. "Your uncle only sent a missive."

"But what is in the missive?" Madalene questioned.

"There is only one way to find out," Isabella encouraged, tugging her towards the door.

Madalene felt trepidation in her heart as she headed towards the dining room of her family's London townhouse, Windham Hall, knowing she would be forced to speak to her odious uncle, the Earl of Stafford. He had summoned her home from Miss Bell's Finishing School in Bath, but fortunately he hadn't been home when she arrived early last night.

She stopped outside the open door and smoothed out her black crepe gown, hoping to delay the inevitable. She had no idea why she was to return home. The missive just stated that she *was* to return home immediately.

"Are you all right, Lady Madalene?" the kind, aging butler asked from behind her.

She turned around and gave him a timid smile. "I'm just gathering up courage," she found herself admitting.

Mr. Hayward's stoic expression gave nothing away, but she saw compassion creep into his eyes.

Taking a step closer, she lowered her voice. "Do you know why my uncle summoned me home?"

"I do not."

Wincing, she glanced over her shoulder at the door. "I suppose I should go in there," she said reluctantly.

"You just turned eighteen years old. Perhaps he plans to present you for the Season," Mr. Hayward suggested.

Glancing down at her gown, she replied, "But it hasn't even been a year since Father and Mother died."

Tenderly, Mr. Hayward placed a hand on her shoulder. "Have courage, Lady Maddie," he remarked affectionately. It was a phrase he'd repeated to her often since her parents' death.

"Thank you, Hayward," she responded. "What would I have done without you?"

His eyes twinkled with humor. "Most likely, you would have gotten into more scrapes."

"That's true. You were always there to pick me back up."

"And I always will be." With a smile on his lips, he dropped his arm and took a step back. "Now off with you," he encouraged. "I made sure the cook made all of your favorites this morning for breakfast."

"Does that include chocolate and bacon?"

He winked. "Of course, milady."

"You should have told me that at the beginning of our conversation. Then I wouldn't have spent as much time chattering on with you out here," she teased, spinning on her heel.

As she walked into the dining room, Madalene took a moment to admire the burgundy wallpaper and antique furniture that her mother had personally selected. This room had so many wonderful memories of her parents. From a young age, she'd had breakfast with them each morning, followed by riding with her father.

Her uncle was sitting at the head of the table with a paper in his hand. He was a tall man with dark, thinning hair, and his bold nose appeared to have grown since the last time she saw him.

"Good, you're finally awake," Lord Stafford said, placing the folded newspaper onto the table.

Stepping to the buffet, Madalene admitted, "I've been awake for a few hours now. I woke up earlier and noticed what a fine day it was, so I went riding."

"Did you have an escort with you?" he asked, censure in his voice.

"I didn't think one was necessary since I stayed on our lands."

"That was foolhardy," her uncle admonished. "From now on, I would like to be notified before you take a ride."

"May I ask why?" she asked, walking over to the table and sitting across from him.

Her uncle lifted his brow at her pertinence. "I'm your guardian, and I am responsible for you."

"I assure you that the woodlands surrounding Windham Hall are safe," she countered.

Placing his arm on the table, he leaned forward and snapped, "You will not defy me on this, Madalene."

"I understand, Uncle," she replied, averting her gaze. She had learned a long time ago that it was best not to argue with him. He would only become more irate.

"Good," he said with a bob of his head. "I hope your return trip from your ladies' finishing school was uneventful."

"It was," she replied, picking up her fork.

"I'm relieved you are safely home where you belong," Lord Stafford remarked, his words sounding insincere.

"Am I to assume that I will not be returning to school?"

He stared at her as if she was a simpleton. "You are eighteen years old. Why would you wish to continue your schooling?"

"I have many dear friends at the school, and I enjoy learning," she admitted.

"You should consider your words carefully. I would hate to think that my niece is a bluestocking," he said sternly.

Madalene placed her fork down and reached for her cup of chocolate. She needed something to calm her nerves and sipping chocolate always did the trick. Why did Society frown on women obtaining an education? To her, that seemed rather daft.

Her uncle pushed back his chair and walked over to the window. He stared out towards the gardens for a long moment. "You may have wondered why I summoned you home before the Season has begun."

"The question may have crossed my mind," she lied, returning her cup to the saucer. She had thought of little else since she got his missive.

Turning, he met her gaze and announced, "I have arranged an advantageous marriage for you."

She stared back at him, stunned into silence. How could he do this to her?

Taking her silence for acceptance, he continued, "It is to Lord Powis's son, Viscount Tattershell."

"But it hasn't even been a full year since my parents' deaths," she reminded him.

"It has been nearly eleven months." He waved his hand dismissively. "That is sufficient time to mourn for one's dead."

It had not escaped her notice that her uncle hadn't mourned her parent's deaths, except for the black armband around his sleeve that he'd worn only during the funeral.

"I don't want to marry Lord Tattershell."

Madalene didn't like the way he looked at her, with pity in his eyes.

"You have no choice." He sighed. "The contract has already been signed."

"You signed the contract without asking me?"

He ran his finger along the windowsill. "You're eighteen and are starting to become a strain on my household."

"A strain?" she repeated. "Is that what you consider me?"

Lord Stafford huffed. "Come, child. You shall be a

viscountess on your wedding day and will one day become the Countess of Powis. You should be thanking me for such a union as this."

"Titles mean very little to me. Besides, I refuse to marry a man that I do not hold in some affection."

"That is rubbish," he humphed. "Marriages are designed to supply an heir; affection has nothing to do with it."

"But I have never met Lord Tattershell."

"It matters not. You will marry him."

Madalene squared her shoulders defiantly. "I will not."

Closing the distance between them in a few strides, he loomed over her. "If you do not marry Lord Tattershell, then I shall banish you from Windham Hall and disown you."

"This is my home!" she exclaimed.

"No," he said with a shake of his head. "This is *my* home, and *you* are but a guest in it."

She rose from her chair. "Then I shall leave at once."

"By all means, go," he encouraged with a flick of his wrist. "However, you shall leave all your clothing, personal effects, and jewelry behind."

"You would keep my clothing?" she asked in disbelief. "For what…"

Her uncle cut her off. "Everything you own belongs to the estate. To *me*."

"That is not accurate," she objected. "My mother gave me her jewelry…"

"No. It all belongs to me!"

She gasped. Her mother's jewelry was the only thing she had of her mother's possessions. She couldn't leave those behind. A thought occurred to her. "May I buy them from you?"

"With what money?" he scoffed.

"Didn't my father leave me some type of inheritance?"

Lord Stafford chuckled dryly. "No. He left you nothing."

"Nothing?" she repeated. How was that possible? How could her parents have left no provisions for her?

"Your parents died unexpectedly, and they had not updated their will since you were young," her uncle explained. "Your father did have the foresight to set aside an account with a generous dowry of £30,000 for you."

Madalene slowly lowered herself back onto the chair. She was trapped. If she left today, she had nowhere to go and no money. Perhaps she could become a governess. She was more than qualified. However, that would take time for her to arrange. She would need to contact an agency or respond to advertisements in the newspaper.

"A garden party is being held in your honor in four days' time, after which, the banns shall be posted," her uncle explained, breaking into her musings.

"In four days?" she asked, incredulous.

His lips twisted into a devious smile. "If you do decide to marry Lord Tattershell, then you will be allowed to take all your possessions, including certain pieces of your mother's jewelry with you as a gift."

"That is most generous of you," she muttered as her mind attempted to formulate a plan of escape. One of her mother's friends would surely help her, but which one?

"Since you are eighteen now, I have made arrangements for you to have a companion," her uncle said, waving someone into the room. "Mrs. Turner is a very capable woman."

Madalene turned towards the door. An older woman, her brown hair peppered with grey, entered the room. Her bun was tied so tightly on top of her head that it pulled her skin upward, and her drab dress seemed to hang on her thin frame.

"Until you're married, she will be responsible for overseeing your education…"

"My education?" Madalene questioned.

Her uncle nodded. "To be an accomplished wife, you must be

proficient at needlework, running a household, playing various instruments, fluent in multiple languages…"

"I already excel at all those things, Uncle."

"We shall see," was his curt response. "I assured Lord Tattershell that you are not lacking in any of those areas."

"I have yet to have a Season," she tried, hoping that her uncle would see reason. "Would it be permissible to wait and post the banns at the end of the Season?"

He shook his head. "The whole point of a Season is to snare a husband. Why would I spend a small fortune to prepare you for the Season when I already procured you a husband?"

Drat! Think, she thought. How else could she delay the engagement?

"Except for riding lessons with the head groomsman, you will not be allowed to go riding," her uncle stated.

"But, Uncle…"

He spoke over her. "I would hate for you to break your pretty neck before your wedding."

With a side glance at Mrs. Turner, Madalene said, "I assure you that I am an accomplished rider…"

"And I assure you that I do not care." Lord Stafford glared at her, and she shuddered involuntarily. "Once you're married to Lord Tattershell, your usefulness to me will expire. So, I urge you to not disappoint me, child."

Before she could reply, Mrs. Turner was at her side, gripping her arm. "Come," she ordered. "We have much to do today, including dressing you in more lively colors."

Madalene rose and followed her new companion out of the dining room. She wasn't a simpleton. Her uncle was forcing her into a marriage with Lord Tattershell, by any means necessary, and she had just become a prisoner in her own home.

How was she going to get herself out of this mess?

2

Everett, the Marquess of Northampton, hated scheming mothers. They were bloody everywhere. He couldn't seem to escape them and their title-hungry daughters, which is why he was currently hiding behind the thick maroon drapes in the Duke of Carmarthen's library.

"Mother, I don't see Lord Northampton," a young woman whined from inside the room.

"Well, keep looking," a matronly voice replied. "I saw him leave the cards room, heading in this direction."

"Perhaps he went back to the ballroom."

"Let's hope not," the older woman said, her voice fading as they hurried down the hall.

Everett heaved a sigh of relief. At twenty-nine, he was a confirmed bachelor, and enjoyed the freedom that came along with not having a wife. He knew he would eventually need to settle down with a young woman and produce an heir, but he had no intention of getting shackled to the first woman who tried to trap him.

He waited to ensure the insipid women were gone before

turning towards the window and pushing it open. After he climbed through the window, he headed towards the gardens, blatantly ignoring all the women that fluttered their eyelashes at him. As he stepped through the rear entrance of the dreadfully warm ballroom, he noted the three golden chandeliers that hung from the domed ceiling, all with hundreds of lighted candles.

He tugged on his cravat, but it did little to cool him off. Women kept glancing his way with coy smiles, hoping to curry favor with him. Why did he attend these blasted events? He already knew that answer. His mother. Somehow, she always managed to convince him to attend.

Breaking through the hordes of his admirers, Penelope, the Duchess of Blackbourne, approached him and teased, "I know that look. Who attempted to trap you?"

Everett shuddered. "It was Lady Rowlings and her awful daughter, Miss Wellburn."

"How did you manage to escape?"

"I hid behind the drapes in the library." A servant walked by with a tray of champagne, and he reached out to grab a flute, downing it in one gulp.

"Have you considered hiring a companion to help safeguard your virtue?" Penelope teased.

He smiled. "Perhaps. It may come to that."

A deep chuckle came from behind him. "Or you could just find a wife and be done with all this nonsense," Nicholas, the Duke of Blackbourne, stated as he stepped up next to his wife.

The duke and duchess exchanged a look that was filled with undeniable love as he slipped his arm around her waist. It was wholly inappropriate to show such displays of affection amongst the *ton*, but Nicholas had never concerned himself with what other people deemed appropriate. That was one of the things Everett liked about his friend.

The dark-haired duke turned back towards him and said, "I

have only been married for a little more than two months now, and I find that I can highly recommend it."

"Not everyone has marital bliss," Everett commented, his eyes scanning the ballroom.

Nicholas nodded. "True."

"You are a marquess and extremely wealthy," Penelope said. "You are the prize of the Season."

"Of every Season," he corrected. "Women have been trying to entrap me since I inherited my title at twenty-two."

Penelope smiled. "I've heard that young women have started carrying around portrait miniatures of you."

He tossed up his hands in frustration. "It's not just the portrait miniatures that irk me. I wish the morning papers would stop speculating about my life. It's exhausting to read about myself nearly every morning."

"How tiring that must be, to be adored by the *ton*," Penelope joked.

"You could go and get yourself a ward like I did," Nicholas suggested.

"If I recall, you weren't pleased when you discovered you had a ward in the first place," he reminded his friend.

"True, but I came to my senses before it was too late," Nicholas stated, sharing a private smile with his wife.

Everett couldn't believe the change that had come over his once gruff and aloof friend, and it was all because of Penelope. Regardless, he had seen too many loveless marriages to know that Nicholas's marriage was the exception.

"I think I am going to bow out and take my leave," he said, placing his empty flute on the tray of a passing servant.

Penelope frowned. "We haven't even had the dinner dance yet."

A few women had edged their way closer and were smiling unabashedly at him. He stifled the urge to groan. "I'm afraid I am not in the mood to dance this evening," he admitted.

Nicholas stepped over and clasped his shoulder. "Would you care to go riding with me tomorrow?"

"It will have to be early because my mother is forcing me to attend the Earl of Powis's garden party tomorrow afternoon. The rumor is that his son, the Viscount of Tattershell, will announce his engagement."

"How awful for you. Another party," Penelope murmured teasingly. "Do you know who Lord Tattershell is expected to marry?"

Everett shrugged. "I'm afraid I don't know."

"Well, I pity the poor girl," Nicholas replied. "Lord Tattershell has a reputation for debauchery. I heard that he is a frequent visitor at the gambling halls across town."

Penelope lifted her brow. "And where did you hear that, husband?"

"At White's," he shared.

"Yet you don't know who he is engaged to?" Everett joked.

Nicholas chuckled. "Trust me. That is all I care to know."

The waltz was announced as the next set, and the men in the room eagerly went to secure their dance partners.

"That is my cue to leave," Everett declared, giving them a mock salute.

As he headed towards the front of the ballroom, an older woman stepped in front of him, effectively halting his retreat.

"Lord Northampton," she started in a loud, cheery voice, "how are you this evening?"

"I am well, but if you will excuse me," he said, attempting to brush past her.

Moving with him, the woman tried again. "Have you met my daughter, Miss Devlin?"

A young woman suddenly appeared by her side. She was attractive enough, but then she smiled, revealing her snaggletooth.

Keeping his face passively inscrutable, Everett bowed. "It is a pleasure to meet you, Miss Devlin."

The older woman's eyes lit up as if she just came up with a marvelous idea. "You know… my daughter does not have a dance partner for this set."

"I'm afraid I do not dance the waltz."

"Oh, that's too bad," the woman pouted. "Perhaps the dinner dance then?"

With an apologetic smile to Miss Devlin, he replied, "It shall have to be another time. I have urgent business I must attend to tonight."

"I look forward to it," Miss Devlin said in a timid voice.

Everett nodded his acknowledgement before he stepped around the woman and headed towards the main entrance. Once he stepped outside, he enjoyed the nice breeze as he proceeded to walk down the long line of coaches until he found his.

A liveried footman was standing in front of the coach door.

"Have you been standing guard all night, Geoffrey?" he asked.

The footman nodded. "I have, Lord Northampton."

"Any unwanted visitors?"

"No, milord."

"Would you still mind checking?"

Reaching for the handle, the footman opened the coach door, and peered inside. Immediately, he said, "It appears that you have entered the wrong coach, miss. May I assist you out?" He stepped to the side and put his hand out.

A gloved hand accepted Geoffrey's assistance before he saw Miss Wellburn exit the coach.

Keeping his face cordial, he bowed. "My apologies, Miss Wellburn. It appears that you were directed to the wrong coach this evening."

"It would appear so, my lord," she replied with a coy smile.

Directing his next comment to Geoffrey, he asked, "Would you mind assisting Miss Wellburn inside? It isn't safe for a woman of her station to be outside unaccompanied."

Stepping closer to him, Miss Wellburn purred, "That's so thoughtful of you."

"Good evening, Miss Wellburn," he said as he stepped into the coach.

For good measure, he latched both doors before he rested his head back against the plush bench. It was exhausting to constantly be on one's guard. He'd even had to hire guards to patrol his estate to prevent women from sneaking into his bedchamber.

Perhaps he should just pick a woman to marry. It would be much simpler that way. Although, he did want to hold his wife in some affection. Not love. That was a rare commodity to have, but he did hope he and his future wife would have mutual respect and appreciation for each other. A true partnership.

It was evident that Nicholas and Penelope deeply loved each other, but they were the exception, not the rule. The *ton* was made up of unharmonious marriages. His parents' union was like most in Society. His father maintained a mistress while in Town, and his mother pretended to be blissfully unaware of the other woman. Frankly, it disgusted him that his father treated his mother so callously.

Regardless, a wife would only complicate matters. And he preferred the life of a bachelor.

Sitting at the head of his spacious dining table, Everett enjoyed the silence as he read his morning newspaper. Most of the articles detailed the success and failures of the Napoleonic

Wars, but one article referenced the skirmish occurring over in America.

"Morning, Son," his mother, the Marchioness of Northampton, said as she stepped into the dining room.

He lowered the paper and took a moment to study his mother, recognizing that time had been exceptionally kind to her. She was still a handsome woman with soft features, and her faded brown hair was swept up into a high chignon, although, he noticed traces of dark circles under her eyes.

"Did you not sleep well, Mother?"

She frowned. "What an awful thing to say to your mother."

"I apologize," he said, finding himself concerned with her tired eyes. "I am surprised you decided to join me for breakfast since you usually eat up in your bedchamber."

"Not today. I decided I wanted to spend time with my son," she said with a smile.

"Ah, lucky me." He brought the paper back up as she came and sat on the right side of the table.

She sighed.

Rather than respond, Everett continued to read his newspaper.

His mother sighed again, this time more dramatically than before.

Slowly, he lowered the newspaper. "Is there something I can do for you, Mother?"

"Yes," she replied. "I want grandchildren."

Ignoring his mother's all-too-familiar proclamation, he brought the paper back up and returned to reading the articles on the Napoleonic Wars.

"Did you not hear me?" his mother asked.

Not bothering to lower the paper, he responded, "I did, but I am choosing to ignore you." He paused before adding, "If you truly want grandchildren, Isabella is nearly eighteen. Perhaps she will give you some grandchildren."

"Isabella is away at finishing school."

"I would be happy to arrange a marriage for her," he suggested.

"You will not," Lady Northampton replied firmly. "Isabella will be presented next Season, and she will be allowed to pick her own suitor."

"And what of Hudson and Dudley?"

He could hear the exasperation in his mother's voice. "Hudson is busy working as a barrister, and Dudley is serving in His Majesty's Royal Navy."

A footman walked over and placed a cup of tea and a plate with two pieces of toast in front of the Marchioness.

Blessed silence descended over them.

"I won't be traveling home with you from Lord Powis's estate today," his mother revealed after a moment.

He hadn't expected that delightful piece of information. Folding the paper, he laid it down on the table, now giving her his full attention. "May I ask why?"

"After the garden party, a few of the other women and I will be going to Gunther's Tea Shop for some of that brilliant lemon ice."

He sighed in relief. "If I am not escorting you home, then there is no reason for me to attend the festivities."

"On the contrary, that is why you should attend."

"I'm not following your logic, Mother."

She reached for her teacup. "You shall have the freedom to socialize with your friends."

"I don't have any friends attending the garden party."

"Pity," she replied, taking a sip. "You need more friends."

Pinching the bridge of his nose, he stifled a groan. Was he truly having this conversation with his mother?

After a long moment, Lady Northampton reached over and placed her hand on his sleeve. "Did you hear me, Everett?"

He lowered his hand and replied, "Yes, I did, but I didn't

want to dignify that with a response since I do have friends. I've just been rather busy handling the affairs of our estate up north."

"You have been working much too hard lately," his mother contended.

"You know spring and summer are exceptionally busy times. Furthermore, my presence is required in Parliament."

"All the more reason for you to enjoy yourself at the garden party today."

Everett frowned. "I have ledgers I must attend to…"

She spoke over him. "And they will be there tomorrow as well."

"Is there a particular reason you would like me to attend besides to make new friends?" he asked sarcastically.

"Perhaps," she replied innocently, "you will find yourself a wife."

He pushed back his chair and rose. "I shall be in my study."

"Wait, don't go."

"I have no intention of marrying at this time, Mother," he remarked. "I am only twenty-nine."

With sad eyes, she said, "I'm just worried about you, Everett."

"You need not concern yourself about me," he assured her.

"I am your mother," she declared, straightening in her chair. "I shall always concern myself with you."

Feeling an overwhelming need to be done with this ridiculous conversation, Everett headed towards the door, but stopped when his mother asked, "You will escort me to Lord Powis's estate, won't you?"

Everett closed his eyes. How he hated social gatherings. He cringed at the thought of socializing with scheming mothers and their dreadful daughters. On the other hand, he *had* promised his mother that he would escort her to the garden party. Blast it! Sometimes he hated being a dutiful son.

Through clenched teeth, he replied, "Yes, but I will not stay for long."

"Excellent." He could hear the smile in her voice.

Everett headed through the grand marble entry hall towards his study. His mother had always hinted that he needed to find a wife, but she had never spoken so boldly about it until today.

Striding into his study, he sat down at his desk, opened a ledger, and attempted to get some work done. But he couldn't seem to concentrate, so he slammed the book shut. A deep chuckle came from the doorway.

"I know that look," his friend, Nicholas, said. "You're frustrated."

"I am," he replied, shoving the ledger to the side. "My mother is now pressuring me to marry."

Nicholas walked further into the room. "Lady Northampton has been dropping subtle hints for years."

"True, but this morning she asked for grandchildren."

"My, that is bold." Nicholas grinned. "What did you say?"

"Nothing. What could I say to that?" He leaned back in his seat and observed his friend. Nicholas had an air of happiness about him. "I can't seem to wrap my mind around how much you have changed since your wedding."

Tugging down on his green riding jacket, the duke replied, "For the first time in many years, I am truly happy. And it is all because of Penelope."

"Do you still frighten little children?" he joked.

Nicholas rubbed his chin thoughtfully. "Not recently."

"I'm pleased that you and Penelope found one another," Everett said, rising from his seat. "I daresay I won't be as lucky."

"You will."

"I highly suspect that won't be the case."

Nicholas leaned his shoulder against the wall. "Love is not something you go out and look for. Love finds you."

"That is rubbish," Everett muttered.

"Falling in love with Penelope was the best thing to ever happen to me," the duke shared.

Everett smiled faintly. "I don't doubt that, but true love is rare. It doesn't just fall from the sky."

"It could."

Laughing, Everett replied, "Enough of this sentimental talk. Let's go riding."

3

Dressed in a white gown with a round neckline, Madalene maintained her smile as she waited for her betrothed to arrive for the garden party. He was already an hour late for the festivities. From her vantage point in the Earl of Powis's drawing room, she could see everyone assembled along the north lawn, waiting patiently for the guests of honor.

Lady Powis sat on a settee, with a cup of tea in her hand. "I daresay I don't know what is keeping our son," she said with an apologetic smile.

Standing next to the drink cart, Lord Powis remarked, "My son is usually much more punctual."

"We aren't concerned, are we, Madalene?" Lord Stafford replied before taking a sip of his brandy.

"No, Uncle," she responded in a submissive tone.

For the past four days, she had attempted to plan her escape, but to no avail. Mrs. Turner was like a leech; she remained close and sucked the fun out of every activity. Because of this, she hadn't had the time to write letters to any agencies about governess positions. The only time Mrs. Turner left her alone was when she was using the privy or sleeping.

Madalene rested her head against the cold windowpane. How was she going to get herself out of this arrangement? She couldn't just flee from Windham Hall with nothing but the clothes on her back. She needed to find employment quickly.

A black coach appeared in the distance. This must be Lord Tattershell, she thought, as she watched the coach approach the estate. It came to a stop near the front entrance, and a footman rushed to open the door.

However, once the door was open, no one exited the coach. Was it empty? After a long moment, a blonde-haired man with a rounded face and thin mustache stepped out, rather stumbled out. As his feet touched the ground, he staggered back against the coach. She could see his wrinkled white shirt was untucked under his unbuttoned waistcoat, and his cravat was untied. His ruddy face held a blank expression as he stared at the estate.

Her uncle came to stand next to her. "That's Lord Tattershell," he acknowledged.

Madalene closed her eyes in mortification. Her betrothed was not only late to the garden party being held in their honor, but he was drunk.

A footman placed his arm around Lord Tattershell's shoulder and escorted him towards the estate.

"Allow me to go retrieve my son," Lord Powis growled before he disappeared from the room.

Turning to face her uncle and struggling to keep her anger in check, she managed to keep her voice low. "Surely, you do not expect me to marry a man that arrives at his own engagement party inebriated."

"I do," he replied sternly as he left the room.

She heard loud shouting coming from the entry hall. Lord Powis was yelling at his son for showing up drunk. In response, Lord Tattershell exclaimed, "I never wanted to marry the chit anyway. I just need her dowry."

Pressing her lips together, Madalene glanced over at Lady

Powis, who was watching her with pity in her eyes. It was terribly embarrassing. Lord Tattershell didn't even want to marry her. He had just made it abundantly clear that he only cared about her dowry, not about her.

A few moments later, Lord Powis shoved his son into the drawing room. Lord Tattershell fell to the ground and laid there for a moment. He wasn't moving, and Madalene hoped that he had fallen asleep. But it was not her lucky day. Her betrothed managed to rise to his knees, raised his head, and his blood-shot eyes scanned the room until they landed on her.

"Is that her?" he asked, his words slurring together.

Lady Powis placed her teacup on the table. "That is Lady Madalene. She is your betrothed."

Nodding, Lord Tattershell rose awkwardly and slowly made his way over to her. He stopped in front of her, looked over his shoulder at his father, and shouted, "She's prettier than I expected!"

Good heavens! Was that supposed to be a compliment? Remembering what was expected of her, she curtsied. "It is a pleasure to meet you, Lord Tattershell."

He laughed. "You are proper. Aren't you?"

"I try to be," she responded.

Lord Tattershell took a step closer to her, and she could smell the alcohol on his breath. His eyes roamed her face. "You will do, Sarah."

Sarah? Did he just call her the wrong name?

Lady Powis spoke up, hastily. "Dear, your betrothed's name is Madalene."

"Mad… a… lene," Lord Tattershell stammered. "It's too long. Why do you have such a long name?"

"It's a family name," she replied.

Placing a hand on her shoulder, he leaned into her. "I like the name Sarah better." He burped. "May I call you Sarah?"

Lord Powis came to stand next to his son. His tone was stern. "Her name is Lady Madalene, Andrew. Not Sarah."

"I know that, Father!" Lord Tattershell shouted. He turned back and smiled flirtatiously at her, revealing a row of rotting teeth. "How about we seal this union with a kiss?"

Her eyes grew wide, and she took a step back, but her escape was stopped by the wall behind her. He couldn't possibly be serious.

"I would prefer not to," she managed to say.

"You're no fun," he joked, his eyes fixated on her lips.

Lord Powis put a hand on his son's shoulder. "Once you are married, you will have plenty of opportunities to kiss Lady Madalene."

She felt like gagging at Lord Powis's words. Lord Tattershell was not entirely awful to look at, but she found his drunkenness revolting. She had no desire to ever kiss this man.

Unexpectedly, Lord Tattershell slipped his arm around her waist and tugged her against him. He pressed his lips tightly against hers, despite her best effort to squirm away. After a moment, he released her and stepped back.

"I've had better, Margaret," he complained, licking his lips. "I need to teach you how to kiss properly. You're too stiff."

"Madalene, dear," his mother corrected.

Wiping her lips off with her white glove, Madalene swallowed hard, afraid she might vomit. His breath reeked of cigars and alcohol, and he had a foul stench emanating from his person. It almost smelled as though he'd bathed in excrement.

With pleading eyes, she sought out her uncle for help, but he stood with a grin on his face. Apparently, he found Lord Tattershell's antics amusing.

"Your guests are waiting, Son," Lady Powis prodded.

Extending his arm, Lord Tattershell leered at her. "Shall we?"

She reluctantly took his arm and allowed him to lead her out to the north lawn, but the moment they stepped onto the grass,

Lord Tattershell dropped her arm and hurried over to a group of men, leaving her standing alone.

Lady Powis stepped up next to her. "I apologize for my son," she started. "He is rather anxious to get married."

"It would almost appear that he doesn't want to marry me," Madalene replied, watching as Lord Tattershell accepted two flutes of champagne from a servant.

"That's nonsense," Lady Powis responded with a shaky breath. "He is just… overwhelmed."

Madalene lifted her brow. "Overwhelmed?"

Stepping closer, Lady Powis lowered her voice. "As wives, we must allow our husbands the freedom that their souls crave, and we must do so without complaint."

"Are you saying that I shouldn't be angry that my betrothed not only arrived drunk to the garden party that was being held in our honor, but that he abandoned me at the first opportunity?"

Lady Powis nodded. "That is precisely what I'm saying."

A servant appeared with a tray of champagne, but Madalene declined. She needed all of her wits about her. Somehow, she needed to find a way to escape, preferably before the announcement of her engagement to Lord Tattershell.

Lady Powis broke through her musings. "Your uncle mentioned you went to Miss Bell's Finishing School."

For the first time in days, Madalene smiled. "I did."

"Then you must know, Penelope, the Duchess of Blackbourne."

Madalene froze. "Penelope married her guardian?"

"She did, and it is a love match," Lady Powis stated. "They've been married for nearly two months now."

Keeping her face expressionless, Madalene asked, "Is the Duchess of Blackbourne in Town for the Season?"

"She is. In fact, I just saw her last evening at the Duke of Carmarthen's ball."

"That's wonderful, wonderful news," Madalene breathed, finally feeling a bit of hope, but it was mixed with trepidation.

"It is," Lady Powis confirmed.

"I shall look forward to seeing my dear friend again," Madalene said as she bobbed her head.

With a solemn expression, Lord Powis walked over to her. "It's time to make the announcement."

Oh no, that would not do. Madalene needed to find a way to escape this gathering and hitch a ride over to Penelope's townhouse. She had no doubt that her friend would help her. Think, she told herself. Suddenly, a stroke of genius came to her.

Leaning closer to Lord Powis, she whispered, "Do you mind if I use the privy before the announcement?"

"Of c… course not," Lord Powis stammered, refusing to make eye contact with her.

Rushing towards the door, her uncle appeared out of the crowd and grabbed her arm. "Where do you think you're going?"

"To the water closet," she whispered, averting her gaze.

"Ah," Lord Stafford said, dropping her arm. "Well, make it quick."

Entering the estate, Madalene rushed down a narrow hall. She kept glancing over her shoulder to be sure no one was following her. Ignoring the curious glances of the servants, she passed the water closet and headed towards the main entrance. Once outside, she picked up her skirts and ran towards the cover of the trees that lined the road.

As she headed deeper into the woods, she realized she needed to formulate a plan, and quickly. It was only a matter of time before her uncle and Lord Tattershell came looking for her. Unfortunately, she had no idea where Penelope's townhouse was located, and she only had a few coins in the reticule tied around her wrist.

The sound of an approaching curricle could be heard coming

from the estate. Her eyes spotted the lone driver as he leisurely drove along the dirt road. He had dark-blonde hair, sharp features, and was dressed as a gentleman. Perhaps he would be willing to provide her with the short ride into London.

The terrifying thought came to her that he might be a friend of Lord Tattershell's. And if that was the case, he would drive her right back to the estate. It would probably be best if she kept her identity a secret until they arrived in Town, assuming she could convince him.

Up ahead, a low hanging branch hung out over the road. What if she climbed the tree and dropped down into the curricle? That way she wouldn't risk being out in the open, and she would have the element of surprise.

Without a better plan in mind, Madalene raced towards the tree and started climbing.

Everett leaned back against the plush bench of his curricle. He had decided to leave before the engagement announcement, much to his mother's dismay. He had mingled politely amongst the other aristocrats, but he felt no joy. They always spoke of the same mundane polite topics, such as hunting and the war.

Suddenly, something fell out of the tree, causing the curricle to tip to one side. Turning, he saw a young woman dressed in a slightly soiled white gown.

He yanked back on the reins. "What is the meaning of this?" he roared in outrage.

Ignoring his question, she placed her hand on the back of the curricle and looked back at Lord Powis's estate.

"Miss… whatever your intentions are, I assure you that you will be greatly disappointed."

She turned to face him, and his breath hitched at the young

woman's undeniable beauty. She had dark brown hair piled high atop her head, which highlighted her small jawbone and full cheeks.

"I must ask you to step down from my curricle," he commanded.

She looked at him with hopeful eyes. "Are you familiar with the Duchess of Blackbourne?"

He eyed her suspiciously. "I am."

"Do you know where their townhouse is located?"

"I do," he confirmed.

She breathed a sigh of relief. "I am a friend of the Duchess. Will you drive me to their townhouse?" She fumbled with the reticule around her wrist. "I can pay you. I have a few coins…"

She spoke with panic in her voice, causing him to act. This young woman clearly needed help, and he was obligated as a gentleman to help her.

"No compensation is needed, miss."

When she smiled, her whole face lit up, transforming her into the most beautiful creature he had ever seen.

"Thank you, sir."

Her smile was infectious, and he almost returned it. *Almost.* Instead, he urged his horses forward and chided himself for agreeing to drive this woman into Town. If anyone saw them together, the implication could be disastrous. Did she only want a ride, or was this a ploy to entrap him? He wasn't entirely sure.

"May I ask your name?" He glanced over at the young woman.

She shook her head. "It is in your best interest if you do not know my name."

Interesting. "Are you a friend of Lord and Lady Powis?"

Again, she shook her head. "No. I just met them today."

"But you are a friend of the Duchess of Blackbourne?"

This time she bobbed her head. "Yes, I am."

"Will your escort be alarmed when he can't find you?"

She turned and glanced behind them. "Most likely."

"Shall I turn back around?"

"Heavens, no!" she exclaimed. "Please, I must get to the Duchess of Blackbourne's townhouse as quickly as possible."

He took a moment to eye her fine white gown and the coral necklace around her neck. It was clear that this woman belonged in Society.

"May I ask why you must travel to the Duchess of Blackbourne's estate?"

She pursed her lips. "I would prefer not to tell you."

This woman was a puzzle, and he loved puzzles. He decided he might make more progress if he asked different types of questions. "Let's see if I can guess your name."

"Go ahead," the young woman encouraged.

"Do you have a title?"

She frowned. "I would rather not say."

"Have you been presented for the Season?"

"Not yet."

Glancing over at her, he asked, "Why?"

"I just returned home from finishing school."

"What is your age?"

Clasping her hands in her lap, she replied, "I just turned eighteen."

He leaned back against the bench. "You are about my sister's age. She is at Miss Bell's Finishing School in Bath."

"What is your sister's name?" she asked cautiously.

"Isabella Beauchamp."

She gasped. "You are Lady Isabella's brother?" She paused, her eyes roaming his clothing. "That means, you are Lord Northampton."

"I am," he admitted hesitantly.

A wide smile came to her lips. "Your sister and I are dear friends."

"I take it that you went to Miss Bell's Finishing School."

"I did."

Their shoulders brushed up against one another as the curricle hit a rut in the road. When it settled, he said, "Now that you know my name, it's only fair that you share yours."

"I would rather not."

Everett found himself intrigued by her adamant refusal to reveal her name. "Are you in some kind of trouble?"

"You could say that," she replied. "Which is why I'm hoping Penelope will help me out of my current circumstance."

"Which is?"

She arched an eyebrow. "Isabella never mentioned what a busybody you are."

He chuckled. "This is rather a new experience for me. I've never had a beautiful young lady drop out of a tree into my curricle before."

"It was much easier than I anticipated," she shared. "I had to climb the tree and wait for the exact moment to jump. If I'd jumped at the wrong time, I fear I would have broken my leg, or worse."

"Do you often climb trees?"

A mischievous glint came into her eyes. "I do. Don't you?"

"Not since I was at Eton."

"You're missing out on all the fun, my lord."

Hearing her say 'my lord', reminded him that he still didn't know her name. He attempted again. "Will you at least share your given name?"

"I suppose that's fair," she said, glancing over her shoulder, "assuming you can make this curricle go faster."

It was clear that this woman was afraid of someone or something. But what? He urged the team faster and lifted an expectant brow at her.

Tentatively, she admitted, "My name is Madalene."

"Madalene?"

He attempted to recall any occasion where his sister spoke of a friend named Madalene, but he couldn't recall one instance.

"How much further?" Madalene asked as they approached the cobblestone streets of London.

Pointing up ahead, he replied, "Not much longer. The duke's townhouse is on Grosvenor Street."

"Thank you for providing me with a ride," she said, her eyes scanning the bustling pavement.

They rode in silence for a short distance before he attempted to engage her in conversation again. "Will you not confide in me?"

"I cannot," she stated in a resigned tone. "It wouldn't be fair to share my burdens with my rescuer."

"But I'm not just any rescuer, I am Isabella's brother," he pressed.

Shifting towards him, she replied, "You've been very kind to me, but I don't want to make trouble for you, Lord Northampton."

A playful smile came to his lips. "And if I don't mind the trouble?"

Madalene watched him with a solemn expression. "If you hadn't come along when you did, I don't know what would have happened to me. You saved me."

"I just gave you a ride into Town," he said, hoping to downplay the significance of his role.

"No, you helped me escape a life that I did not want."

Reining in his team in front of a stately three-level, red brick structure, with a portico supported by four high columns at the main entry, he announced, "Welcome to Hereford Hall."

"This is where Penelope lives?" she asked with wide eyes.

"It is," he confirmed.

Her gaze roamed over the large estate and its pristine gardens. "It's beautiful."

He exited the curricle and came around to assist her down.

Reaching up, he placed his hands on her waist and slowly lowered her to the ground. Stepping back, he pointed towards the door. "Shall we?"

She stayed rooted to her spot. "I go alone from here."

He tsked. "I think not, my damsel in distress."

"It would be best if you left now and forgot all about me," she pressed. "My name will no doubt be plagued with scandal after tonight."

He shrugged. "I find I like to live dangerously."

Madalene pressed her lips together, clearly displeased by his refusal. "Don't say that I didn't warn you."

Offering his arm, he was pleased when she accepted. "I am still holding out hope that I can discover your identity."

"I fear you shall be disappointed."

Before he knocked on the door, it was open, revealing the butler.

"Lord Northampton, what a pleasure to see you today," he said, opening the door wide.

Stepping into the entry hall, Everett replied, "Thank you, Hawkins. Is the duchess available for callers?"

"She is, my lord." He eyed Madalene. "May I tell her who is calling, miss?"

Her eyes darted towards his before she replied, "Will you just tell her Madalene is calling?"

"As you wish, Miss Madalene," Hawkins said before spinning on his heel and exiting the hall.

As they waited for the butler to return, Everett watched as Madalene's eyes roamed over the painted mauve columns framing the doors and the intricately designed ceiling.

"It's all so beautiful," she murmured.

Everett heard the sound of rushing feet before Penelope turned the corner. When she saw the young woman still holding his arm, a wide smile graced her face. "Madalene!"

Madalene dropped his arm and rushed to embrace her friend.

"I'm so happy that you came to call," Penelope said, looping her arm through hers. "Come, I have ordered us some refreshment in the drawing room." She glanced over her shoulder. "I find myself filled with curiosity, however. Why has Lord Northampton escorted you here?"

"He provided me with a ride to your estate," Madalene shared. "I only just learned that you were in Town for the Season."

"Did you not get my letter?" Penelope asked as Everett followed behind them.

Madalene shook her head. "No, I didn't. My uncle summoned me home."

"I have so much to tell you," Penelope stated.

However, the moment they stepped into the drawing room, to Everett's surprise and horror, Madalene started crying.

Penelope placed an arm around her shoulder. "Whatever is the matter, Maddie?"

"Oh, Penelope! I need your help," she sobbed.

4

Madalene attempted to control her growing emotions, but she was so tired of being strong. For days, she'd been a prisoner in her own home, and finally, she escaped from her uncle's clutches, and now she didn't know what to do.

Except for her mother's coral necklace, she'd escaped with only the clothes on her back and a few coins that she'd kept from her allowance at the finishing school.

"Perhaps it's best if you start from the beginning," Penelope suggested as she guided her over to the settee.

Lord Northampton made his way to another seat on the other side of the room, but before anyone could sit down, a thunderous voice came from the doorway.

"Why do I hear crying?"

"Maddie is crying," Penelope explained, barely sparing the man a glance.

Walking further into the room, the tall, dark-haired man asked, "Who in the blazes is Maddie, and why is she crying in *our* drawing room?"

Penelope turned to face her husband. "Maddie is one of my dearest friends from Miss Bell's Finishing School."

"Does she cry all the time or is this a new behavior?" he asked skeptically.

"I apologize, your grace," Madalene said as she wiped her cheeks with her gloves. "I'm afraid my emotions have gotten the better of me." She curtsied respectfully.

The duke approached her, watching her with a piercing scrutiny that made her anxious. "Why were you crying?"

Glancing over at Penelope, her friend gave her an encouraging nod. "My uncle is attempting to force me into an unwanted marriage, your grace," she shared.

"I see." He continued to glower down on her. "Is it an advantageous marriage?"

"It is."

"Then I'm afraid I don't understand the issue."

Lord Northampton let out a groan. "Blast it, Nicholas. You're scaring the poor girl."

"I am not," he contended. "A woman of her station aspires to…"

"Hush, husband," Penelope interrupted. She stepped over to stand next to him and smiled kindly at Madalene. "You'll have to forgive my husband. He can be a little archaic at times."

"At times?" Madalene heard Lord Northampton mutter under his breath.

"Let's start from the beginning so we can understand Maddie's perspective," Penelope suggested.

The duke nodded his consent as he walked over to the drink cart. He poured two drinks and extended one towards Lord Northampton.

"Lady Madalene Ramsbury, allow me to introduce you to my husband, Nicholas, the Duke of Blackbourne," Penelope said.

The duke gave her a stiff bow before he took a sip of his drink.

Turning her gaze towards Lord Northampton, she saw that his brow was lifted.

"You are a *titled* lady," he said.

"I am."

"And you saw no reason to mention that on the ride over?"

"I did not," she replied boldly.

The duke chuckled as he swirled the brandy in his snifter. "I like this one."

"Will you tell us what you are running away from?" Penelope encouraged.

Madalene clasped her hands in front of her. "My uncle, the Earl of Stafford…"

"The Earl of Stafford is your uncle?" the duke huffed, cutting her off. "I would run away, as well. That man is an imbecile."

"At the risk of seeming impertinent, I agree with you, your grace," Madalene stated. "He summoned me home from finishing school and ordered me to marry Lord Tattershell."

"That was *your* garden party?" Lord Northampton asked, placing his glass onto a side table.

"It was," she confirmed. "My uncle informed me that if I didn't marry Lord Tattershell, then he would kick me out of his estate with only the clothes on my back. He even refused to let me keep my mother's jewelry or any of my personal effects."

"Did he state why?" Penelope asked.

She frowned. "He said that everything I own belongs to the estate."

"Including your clothes?" Lord Northampton pressed.

A maid slipped through the door with a tray in her hands. They watched in silence as she walked further into the room and placed it on the table in front of them.

"That will be all, Rebecca," Penelope said to the maid as she sat down on the settee and reached for a teacup.

Sitting down next to Penelope, Madalene shared, "I haven't even gotten to the worst part yet."

"It gets worse?" Lord Northampton asked, crossing his arms over his chest.

She nodded. "My uncle hired a companion for me that was more like a guard. For the past four days, she has followed me around the estate, ensuring I followed a rigorous studying schedule, and refusing to let me even step outside."

Nicholas took a sip of his drink. "Did your uncle state why he wanted you to marry Lord Tattershell?"

"No. He only mentioned that the contract had already been signed, and that I was a burden on his household," she explained.

Penelope extended her a cup of tea. "Oh, Maddie. I wish you had come to me sooner. How did you even discover I was in Town?"

Madalene accepted the cup and took a sip of the warm drink, and she had to admit that the tea helped soothe her. "Lady Powis informed me just before the engagement announcement. The moment I discovered you were in Town, I used the excuse of having to use the privy and ran out the main door." She took another sip of her tea. "I saw Lord Northampton's curricle leaving the estate, so I climbed up a tree and waited for the right moment to jump in."

"You jumped down into a moving curricle from a tree?" the duke asked, incredulous.

"I did," she replied, smiling a little. "It was my only chance at freedom, so I took it."

His grace gave her an approving nod. "Well done."

Placing her empty cup on the tray, Madalene turned towards Penelope. "I asked my uncle for a Season, but he refused. He said that he saw no reason to spend a small fortune when he had already ensnared a husband for me."

"We shall host a Season for you," Penelope declared.

She shook her head. "No, no, no… I couldn't ask that of you."

"What is it that you want from us, Lady Madalene?" the duke asked.

Strengthening her resolve, Madalene replied, "I intend to

seek employment as a governess, but I need a place to stay until I receive an offer of employment."

The duke and Penelope exchanged a look, but Madalene couldn't decipher the meaning.

"No," the duke surprised her by saying. "You are the daughter of an earl, and it is beneath you to become a governess."

She winced. "I have no other options, your grace. It's either become a governess, or maybe… a street cleaner?" She hoped the joke would lighten the tension in the room.

"A street cleaner?" Lord Northampton repeated in disbelief.

"Frankly, I am not sure what other jobs I am qualified for besides being a governess," she admitted. "I'm proficient at needlework. I suppose I could work in a shop sewing gowns."

"You cannot work in a shop," Penelope admonished.

Madalene lowered her gaze to her lap. "What other choice do I have?"

The duke sat down in an armchair across from her. "Do you have any funds available to you?"

"No," she said with a shake of her head. "Furthermore, I just recently learned that my father's will was outdated, so I inherited nothing from his estate."

"Did the will specify a dowry?" Lord Northampton asked, leaning his shoulder against the wall.

She nodded. "It did. £30,000."

"That's a generous dowry." The duke rubbed his chin thoughtfully. "Have you by chance read the will?"

"No," she admitted.

"It just seems rather odd to me that a mother wouldn't specify some of her jewelry to be willed to her daughter," the duke remarked.

Fingering the coral necklace around her neck, she admitted, "I did abscond with this coral necklace. It was my grandmother's, and it was supposed to be passed down to me."

"I agree with Nicholas," Lord Northampton stated. "What I find peculiar is that Lord Stafford selected Lord Tattershell as your betrothed."

She grimaced. "Lord Tattershell is a horrid man. He arrived over an hour late to the garden party, and he was drunk. At one point, I thought he'd fallen asleep on the carpet." She brought her hands up to her lips as she reluctantly admitted, "And he kissed me in front of his parents and my uncle."

"He kissed you?" Penelope asked.

"Yes," she replied in a hushed tone. "I fear kissing is rather unenjoyable."

A smile came to Penelope's face. "I assure you that kissing is quite enjoyable if you have the right partner."

Madalene shuddered in disgust. "His breath smelt of tobacco and alcohol, and a truly pungent odor emanated from his person."

Lord Northampton pushed off from the wall and went to sit in an armchair near the duke. "No wonder you fled."

"I'd already made the decision to escape, but I was waiting for the right opportunity," she stated.

Penelope reached for her hand and squeezed it. "I am so glad you had the chance."

"Thank you," Madalene responded, feeling so grateful for her friend's support. "I know you are newly married, and I hate to intrude…"

"Nonsense. You're always welcome in our home," the duke interrupted.

A mischievous glint came to Penelope's eyes. "I am very glad you arrived when you did, because I find that I am in desperate need of a companion for the Season."

Knowing what Penelope was attempting to do, Madalene shook her head. "You don't have to hire me. I am content trying to find employment as a governess."

"That's rubbish," Penelope proclaimed. "We shall have all Season to sort out this mess."

Tears came to Madalene's eyes, but she tried to blink them away. "I knew you would help me, Penelope."

Rising, Penelope announced, "Since you only have the clothes on your back, it is time that we go shopping."

"But I don't have any money," she protested.

"But I do." Penelope grinned. "Just consider it an advance on your salary."

"Thank you." With a grateful heart, Madalene rose and embraced her friend.

As she leaned back, Penelope stated, "My pleasure. The ladies of Miss Bell's Finishing School must stick together."

Madalene opened her eyes as the sun streamed through the cracks between the drapes. She smiled as she heard birds chirping merrily outside her window. What a delightful way to be woken up, she thought.

Rolling over in bed, she was shocked to discover a freckled face young woman was staring back at her.

"Good morning, Lady Madalene," the girl said in a cheery voice.

Madalene gasped. "Where did you come from?"

The young woman gave her a curious glance. "From downstairs. Mrs. Seymour, the housekeeper, instructed me to act as your lady's maid for the Season."

Sitting up in bed, Madalene admonished, "I think there must be a mistake. I am only her grace's companion, not her guest."

"Mrs. Seymour informed me of that fact, milady, but she still sent me up here." The maid walked over to the settee by the fireplace and picked up a white gown. "Her grace asked me to alter a few of her gowns to fit you, while we are waiting for your dresses to arrive from the modiste."

"That's most kind of her," Madalene admitted.

The young woman draped the dress over the back of the settee. "The duchess *is* most kind and gracious." She stilled. "Where are my manners?" she asked, curtsying in an exaggerated fashion. "My name is Amy Thrup."

"It's nice to meet you, Miss Thrup."

Amy shook her head adamantly. "Oh no, milady. You may just call me Amy."

"May I ask how old you are, Amy?"

"I just turned sixteen, I did," she answered proudly. "I may be young, but I assure you that I am more than capable of being your lady's maid."

Tossing off her covers, Madalene sat on the edge of the bed. "I have no doubt."

Amy picked up a brush from the dressing table. "Shall we prepare you for the day?"

Madalene rose from the bed. "I suppose we must."

"You sound reluctant."

As Madalene sat down on the chair, she admitted, "I am. I'm not entirely sure what a companion does."

"I believe your job is to entertain her grace."

"If that's the case, then do you happen to know any good jokes?"

Amy stilled. "I believe her grace would be much more interested in you reading to her or helping her with her needlework."

"I happen to know that the duchess does not enjoy embroidery," Madalene said, grinning.

Amy placed the brush down onto the dressing table and started tugging on her hair, twisting and curling it around her fingers. After securing it with pins, she stepped back and cocked her head. "Are you pleased with your hairstyle, Lady Madalene?"

Turning to the side, Madalene admired her hair in the mirror. It was piled high on her head in an intricate fashion. "It's lovely, Amy," she murmured.

Her lady's maid smiled from ear to ear.

Amy walked over to the white gown draped over the settee and held it up for her inspection. "Her grace reminded me that you should only be wearing dresses in white or pale colors."

Madalene took a moment to admire the white muslin gown with ornate embroidery along the neckline. "It's beautiful," she said.

"We must hurry if you would like to join their graces for breakfast."

"The duchess doesn't eat in her room?"

Amy shook her head. "No. They eat breakfast together every morning."

"Perhaps I should just eat in the kitchen to grant them privacy."

Her lady's maid looked baffled. "Why would you do that?"

"Because I am only a companion," Madalene reminded her.

"Her grace requested that you dine with them."

She offered Amy a weak smile. "Then, I suppose I must not disappoint her."

A short time later, Amy escorted Madalene to the family's private dining room. She stopped at an open door and held out her hand, indicating she should enter.

"Thank you, Amy," Madalene murmured as she entered the dining room. The duke sat at the head of the table, and Penelope sat to his right side.

Penelope turned in her chair to greet her. "Good morning, Maddie. How did you sleep last night?"

"Well, thank you."

Madalene approached the buffet table. She placed toast and bacon onto her plate. As she approached the table, a footman pulled out a chair for her.

"What do you intend to do today?" Penelope asked.

Reaching for her napkin, Madalene placed it on her lap as a footman placed a cup of tea and a cup of chocolate in front of her. "I suppose whatever you're doing since I'm your companion."

"That's not necessary. You don't need to follow me around all day," Penelope declared. "Nicholas has a well-stocked library, an impressive collection of horses, and plenty of trees for you to climb."

"Why would Lady Madalene want to climb trees?" Nicholas asked, bewildered.

Penelope grinned. "Maddie used to climb the trees surrounding the finishing school almost every day."

"A lady does not climb trees," Nicholas admonished. "You are welcome to sit under one and read a book, however." He picked the newspaper up off the table and extended it towards her. "It might be best if you avoid doing anything scandalous for the time being."

Madalene accepted the folded paper and saw it was open to the social page. An article was entitled, "*Lady Madalene Ramsbury flees from her fiancé*." Her eyes grew wider as she continued to read the article. Luckily, it made no mention of Lord Northampton.

She placed the newspaper back onto the table in a huff. "I am ruined."

"Yes, you are," Nicholas confirmed.

Penelope shot him a look of exasperation. "My dear, will you please stop being such a naysayer."

"I'm just stating the facts," Nicholas contended.

A man's voice came from the doorway. "You always did have a way with words, Nicholas."

He grunted. "Don't you have your own townhouse to eat at?"

Lord Northampton walked further into the room. "I do. I just wanted to see how the lovely Lady Madalene was faring this morning."

"Awful," she admitted, shifting to face him. "The morning newspaper detailed how I fled from Lord Tattershell. I am utterly ruined."

"Being ruined is relative," Lord Northampton replied.

Reaching for her teacup, she quoted her favorite teacher from school. " 'A woman's greatest asset is her reputation. Without it, she has nothing.' "

"That's balderdash," he proclaimed. "You still have powerful friends that can help you out of this situation."

"How?" she asked curiously.

"I don't know yet." He shrugged. "But I'm not ready to give up. Are you?"

"I am not."

"Good." He walked over to the buffet table and piled food on a plate. "Since I am only a lowly marquess, I was hoping the high and mighty duke would have a few brilliant suggestions."

Nicholas frowned. "For starters, you need to go back to your own townhouse."

Walking closer to the table, Lord Northampton breathed a disappointed sigh. "Fine. It appears that *I* will need to come up with a clever plan to save Lady Madalene."

"Is that even possible?" she pressed.

Lord Northampton placed his plate down on the table and sat down. "The *ton* is mostly a flighty lot. We just have to give the members of Society a chance to adore you."

Turning towards Penelope, she asked, "Do *you* think that is possible?"

Penelope smiled. "I do. I was abducted at a ball by my former business associate, and the *ton* still embraced me."

"That is because you are the Duchess of Blackbourne," she pointed out.

Nicholas spoke up. "That's partially true. No one would dare criticize or belittle my wife or they would have to contend with *me*."

Seeing the undeniable love between Penelope and the duke made Madalene's heart rejoice. It was evident that they were a love match, which is what she aspired to.

Penelope had just picked up her fork to start eating when the butler announced, "Lord Stafford is here to speak to Lady Madalene."

Oh no, he'd found her! She closed her eyes as trepidation filled her heart.

The sound of two chairs being shoved backed caused her to open her eyes. A stoned-face Duke of Blackbourne and an equally solemn Lord Northampton stared back at her.

"Good. I was expecting him," the duke barked, causing her to jump.

"You what?" she asked with an incredulous tone.

Nicholas's eyes grew determined. "I sent word to Lord Stafford that you were residing at Hereford Hall for the time being."

Her mouth gaped in shock. "Why would you do that?"

"As your guardian, he has a right to know that you're safe," he stated simply.

"Would you like me to come with you?" Madalene asked as she began wringing the napkin in her lap.

In a stern tone, the duke replied, "Absolutely not."

"I agree with Nicholas," Lord Northampton stated. "We will speak to your uncle."

Glancing between them, she replied, "I couldn't possibly ask you to do that."

"We weren't asking your permission." Lord Northampton smirked.

Without saying another word, they left the room.

Madalene turned her worried gaze towards Penelope. "Will they be all right?"

"The person you should be worried about is Lord Stafford," Penelope said, reaching for her cup of chocolate.

Leaning back in her chair, Madalene felt her anxiousness begin to disappear. For the first time since her parents died, she felt protected and dare she say… cared for.

5

Everett knew he was scowling, but he didn't care. He was furious about Lord Stafford's treatment of Madalene. He stormed past Nicholas as he strode towards the drawing room. Just as they reached the closed door, Nicholas grabbed his shoulder and yanked him back.

"Northampton, you need to calm yourself," Nicholas said firmly.

Everett raised his eyebrows. "I need to calm myself?"

"I will not have you meet with Lord Stafford if you are acting recklessly."

"Define reckless," he grunted.

Nicholas stepped closer to him and lowered his voice. "We both know that Lord Stafford wronged his niece, but you must always have a battle plan."

"I plan to beat Lord Stafford to a bloody pulp," Everett declared.

"Wrong answer," Nicholas said, stepping back. "Go back into the dining room with the ladies."

He shook his head. "I think not."

"Then you must be rational. We must stay one step ahead of Lord Stafford."

Everett ran a hand through his hair. "I'm not one of your soldiers to command."

"You're right," Nicholas agreed. "You are my friend, and you need to trust me."

Suddenly, the desire to tease his friend was greater than his anger. "Did you just refer to me as your friend?"

The duke huffed. "Why am I friends with such an ignoramus? It's beyond me," Nicholas muttered under his breath as he opened the drawing room door.

Everett followed behind and closed the door, ensuring their conversation would be private.

Lord Stafford stood next to the window, the morning light reflecting off his thinning hair. He turned to face them when they walked into the room and demanded, "Where is my niece?"

"Allow me to introduce myself, Lord Stafford," Nicholas started, "I am the Duke of Blackbourne."

"I know who you are. In fact, everyone knows who you are." Lord Stafford shifted his gaze towards Everett. "And you are Lord Northampton."

"Good, now that the pleasantries are out of the way, we can continue this civil chat," Nicholas grunted.

Lord Stafford crossed his arms over his chest. "I want my niece back."

"No," Nicholas replied without hesitation.

"I will go to the magistrate."

"I won't stand in your way."

Lord Stafford's eyes narrowed. "I will go to the Prime Minister."

Nicolas grinned, unabashed. "Please give my regards to Lord Liverpool."

Uncrossing his arms, Lord Stafford glared at Nicholas. "For what purpose are you keeping my niece?"

"Lady Madalene is a dear friend of my wife's," Nicholas shared.

"I was not aware of that fact," Lord Stafford admitted.

Nicholas walked over to an armchair and sat down. "Were you aware that the duchess went to Miss Bell's Finishing School with your niece?"

Lord Stafford shook his head. "Regardless, I am her guardian, and my niece is rather confused at this time."

"Confused?" Everett asked. "Is she confused because she refuses to marry Lord Tattershell?"

"Madalene agreed to marry Lord Tattershell of her own free will and choice," Lord Stafford asserted.

"Is that why she ran away before the announcement?" Nicholas questioned.

Lord Stafford frowned. "Again, she is just a confused little girl."

"No, she is not a little girl," Everett declared. "Lady Madalene is eighteen, and she is old enough to make her own decisions."

"Clearly she's not, since she ran away, unescorted, to London," Lord Stafford disagreed.

Everett leaned his shoulder against the yellow wallpaper. "She didn't go unescorted. I drove her."

"You abducted my Madalene!" Lord Stafford shouted.

Unperturbed by Lord Stafford's sudden outburst, he replied, "No, she jumped into my curricle to get away from *you*."

"You ruined her."

Everett shook his head. "No, *you* ruined her the moment you agreed that she should marry Lord Tattershell."

Lord Stafford took a commanding step towards him. "You had no right to offer her a ride in your curricle."

"I see it differently," Everett contended with a slight shrug of his shoulder. "I saw a young woman in distress, and I offered to assist her."

Turning his gaze back towards Nicholas, Lord Stafford attempted, "This is all just a misunderstanding. After I speak to Madalene…"

"We have heard some distressing news about your treatment of Lady Madalene," Nicholas said, cutting him off.

"And just what have you heard, your grace?" Lord Stafford drawled.

Nicholas's expression grew thunderous. "I warn you to curb your tongue or this conversation is over." His voice was firm, unyielding.

Lord Stafford visibly shrank back. "My apologies."

"Did you prohibit Lady Madalene from leaving the estate with any of her clothing, personal effects, or her mother's jewelry?" Nicholas asked.

"Everything Madalene owns belongs to me, including the family jewels," Lord Stafford contended.

"Pray tell," Everett asked, "what do you intend to do with women's clothing and accessories?"

"That is none of your concern, Lord Northampton," the earl snapped.

"I disagree," Everett stated, pushing away from the wall. "Lady Madalene is a good friend of my sister's, as well. I am dismayed to hear that you have been treating her so poorly."

Lord Stafford cocked his head. "I arranged for an advantageous marriage to Lord Tattershell. He is a viscount and one day will be the Earl of Powis."

"Lord Tattershell is a scoundrel," the duke stated matter-of-factly. "He is a known rake and frequents gambling dens in and around London."

"What man doesn't dabble in a few vices, gentlemen?" Lord Stafford asked, tugging down on the lapels of his royal blue jacket.

Nicholas slowly rose from his chair. "Based on this enlightening conversation, I have decided that Lady Madalene will remain under my protection."

"But I am her guardian!" Lord Stafford yelled.

Taking a step closer to the earl, Nicholas said, "Bring me the will which states that you are, in fact, Lady Madalene's guardian, and I will release her to you."

Lord Stafford's face went slack. "I don't know where the will is."

"Then find it," Nicholas encouraged.

Turning his gaze towards the window, Lord Stafford tried again. "She's to be married in three weeks. The banns were posted yesterday. If she doesn't marry Lord Tattershell, then you have cursed her to a life of spinsterhood."

"My wife and I intend to present Lady Madalene for the Season," the duke shared.

Lord Stafford scoffed. "That won't save her reputation. She will be gossiped about and criticized at every turn." He grinned cruelly. "You won't be able to protect her from the malicious things that will be said about her behind her back."

Nicholas and Everett exchanged a look, both acknowledging what Lord Stafford was saying was true. Madalene was the latest scandal, and the *ton* loved nothing more than to pounce on scandals.

"Regardless, Lady Madalene will remain with us at Hereford Hall for the time being," Nicholas asserted.

Lord Stafford scowled. "Do you intend to make Madalene your mistress, your grace?"

Closing the distance between them in two strides, Nicholas punched the earl in the jaw, knocking him to the ground. He stood over him and exclaimed, "How dare you make such an outlandish accusation!"

"What will the *ton* think when a disgraced woman is living with you?" the earl asked, holding his reddening jaw.

Everett knew Lord Stafford made a good argument. Madalene was ruined, and the only thing that could save her was the safety of marriage. But marrying Lord Tattershell wasn't an option.

Suddenly, a thought came to him. A thought that would solve all his problems, at least for this Season.

Standing straighter, his jaw set in determination, he proclaimed, "I will marry Lady Madalene."

Nicholas turned to him with a dumbfounded expression. "Pardon?"

"*I* will marry Madalene," he repeated.

"That is unacceptable," Lord Stafford said, rising from the ground. "She's engaged to Lord Tattershell. I would be sued for breach of contract."

Everett stepped over to the drink cart and took the lid off the decanter. "Then, so be it. She is engaged to me, and we will be wed at the end of the Season."

The earl grew silent for a long moment before he tossed his hands up in the air. "Fine! Keep the chit for all I care!" he shouted. "But do I have your word as a gentleman that you will marry her?"

He nodded. "I give you my word, assuming *she* agrees to marry me."

"Of course she'll marry you. You are a marquess," Lord Stafford said in a tone that implied he was a simpleton.

As he poured himself a drink, he asked, "Now about her dowry…"

"Naturally you'd want to talk about something so unsavory at a time like this," the earl grumbled.

"I am aware of Madalene's dowry of £30,000, but was she also left an inheritance from her parents' estate?" Everett inquired.

Lord Stafford visibly stiffened. "No. She was left nothing."

"Not even her mother's jewelry?"

He shook his head. "You must understand that her parents died unexpectedly, and they did not have an updated will."

"May we see the will?" Everett pressed as he gently swirled the snifter in his hand.

With an apologetic shrug, the earl replied, "Again, I don't know where it is."

"Then who was your brother's solicitor?" Nicholas asked. "Perhaps he still has a copy."

"Mr. Simms was my brother's solicitor," Lord Stafford replied, frowning. "I'll send a missive to see if he has a copy of the will."

"Indeed. We're finally getting somewhere," Everett joked.

"Now if you will excuse me, I will go break the bad news to Lord Powis and Lord Tattershell," Lord Stafford said, taking a step towards the door.

"Before you go," Nicholas spoke up, causing Lord Stafford to stop in his tracks. "Would you like me to pass along a message to your niece?"

"I would," Lord Stafford asserted, tugging down on his waistcoat. "Tell her that I will never forgive her for embarrassing me in front of Lord and Lady Powis." He spun on his heel and departed from the room.

Everett chuckled. "That was a tender moment."

Nicholas turned his expectant gaze towards him. "Do you want to explain why you offered for Lady Madalene?"

Everett put his hands up in front of him. "I have no intention of *actually* marrying her."

"Explain, *now*," the duke ordered, his jaw clenched.

"My name is the only thing that will protect Madalene's reputation now," Everett began. "We won't post the banns, but we let the news circulate that we have an understanding between us. It will allow her the freedom to attend balls, soirées, and other social gatherings under the guise of our engagement. If not for our engagement, all those invitations would be rescinded."

Nicholas eyed him warily. "That's true. However, if you don't marry Madalene at the end of the Season… well, no reputation could ever recover from *two* broken engagements."

"True, but with any luck, by the end of the Season, she'll have a long line of suitors vying for her attention," he replied. "I want to give her the Season that her uncle refused."

"This is madness," Nicholas asserted. "I can't even count how many ways this could go horribly, terribly wrong. Then you would have no choice but to marry Lady Madalene."

"I doubt it will come to that," Everett assured his friend.

Nicholas rubbed the sides of his forehead. "What do you hope to gain from all this?"

"Nothing," he lied.

Dropping his hand, his friend met his gaze. "You must be getting something out of this."

Crossing his arms over his chest, Everett replied, "Nothing other than the satisfaction of helping my sister's friend."

"No," Nicholas argued with a shake of his head. "I've known you for most of my life, and you would never have willingly shackled yourself to a woman, especially one that you barely know."

The two men stood in silence for a moment, staring at each other.

Suddenly, Nicholas's eyebrows shot up and he began clapping slowly. "Well done," he said. "By circulating the news that you and Lady Madalene have an understanding, all the scheming mothers will leave you alone for the Season."

"That's an added benefit…"

Nicholas cut him off. "You're still a fool. If your plan fails, you'll have no choice but to marry Lady Madalene."

"That's assuming she wants to marry me," Everett reminded his friend.

"Regardless, I'll ask my solicitor to contact Mr. Simms and

request a meeting to view a copy of the late Earl of Stafford's will."

Adjusting his white cravat, Everett replied, "I have no doubt that Lord Stafford is lying to us, but for what purpose?"

"We'll look into it," Nicholas began, "but now you need to go woo your bride and convince her to go along with this madcap scheme."

Everett glanced at the door. "It shouldn't be too difficult."

Nicholas guffawed. "I wish you luck with that," he said as he departed the room.

Frowning, Everett attempted to ignore Nicholas's laughter as it echoed around the entry hall. He had no doubt that Madalene would see the validity of his plan and agree to it.

Madalene sipped her chocolate as she read the morning newspaper. She couldn't believe the freedoms that she now experienced at Hereford Hall. Her uncle would never have let her read the newspaper, saying it was unladylike. Under the article written about her, there was a piece about Lord Everett Northampton and where he was last sighted. Apparently, he had attended the theatre a few days prior with his mother, Lady Northampton, and was seen talking to Miss Abigail Whipple.

The duke walked into the room with a subdued grin on his face.

"I take it that the meeting went well," Penelope remarked.

Nicholas stepped up to her and leaned close to her ear. He whispered something, causing Penelope to gasp softly.

She turned towards her husband. "He didn't."

"He did," Nicholas confirmed.

Confused and curious, Madalene asked, "What did he do?"

The duke straightened and turned his piercing gaze towards her. "It would be best if Everett told you himself."

"I intend to do so without prying ears," Everett said, walking into the room. He smiled kindly at her. "May I speak to you alone in the drawing room?"

"Of course, Lord Northampton," she murmured, rising from her chair.

He didn't speak as she followed him to the drawing room, and she was surprised when he closed the door behind her.

Everett turned to face her. "How are you settling in here?"

"Very well," she answered. "Although, I feel more like an honored guest than I do a companion."

"That's good, because your circumstances have changed yet again."

Confusion furrowed her brow. "In what way?"

"Would you care to sit down?" Everett gestured towards an ivory camelback settee.

As Madalene sat down, she asked, "How did the meeting go with my uncle?"

"It went well," Everett said, smiling. "He was quite concerned about your well-being."

"He was?" she questioned incredulously. That didn't sound anything like her uncle.

Everett chuckled. "No. He was irate and demanded that you be returned to him. He even threatened to go to the Prime Minister."

That sounds more like my uncle, she thought. "He did?"

"Yes." Everett bobbed his head. "Nicholas responded by telling him to give his regards to Lord Liverpool."

"That was most kind of his grace," she replied.

Everett surprised her by coming to sit down next to her. "Nicholas has a kind heart hidden behind his gruff exterior."

"I know. I've witnessed that. He adores Penelope."

"They are most assuredly a love match."

Being this close to Everett caused Madalene to feel self-conscious. He was a remarkably handsome man with a strong jaw and sharp features. Stop, she chided herself. She had no right to ogle her rescuer.

Unaware of her internal dilemma, Everett shared, "Lord Stafford was adamant that you marry Lord Tattershell."

She shuddered. "I refuse. I failed to mention that he called me by the wrong name multiple times, and even had the audacity to ask if he could call me Sarah."

"Why Sarah?"

"He claimed it was easier to say than Madalene."

Everett let out a deep baritone laugh. "Well, at least he had a reason, albeit a poor one." Then, he grew serious. "You should know that Nicholas requested to see a copy of your father's will."

"Did my uncle agree?"

"No, he did not," Everett replied. "By chance, do you have any idea where your uncle might keep the will?"

"Most likely in his study," she answered, "but he keeps the door locked whenever he isn't home."

Rubbing his chin thoughtfully, Everett stated, "If your uncle doesn't produce the will, then we'll need to find a way into his study."

"How?"

"We'll find a way," he said reassuringly.

Everett angled his body towards her. "Which brings me to another topic that I wish to discuss with you." He hesitated, and he almost appeared nervous. "Your uncle was determined that you marry Lord Tattershell, and I proposed another solution."

"Which was?" she asked, growing anxious.

He met her gaze. "That I marry you."

"No!" she cried, jumping up from her seat. "You cannot be in earnest."

"I am truly in earnest."

"I won't let you do this."

"This is my choice," he said calmly as he rose.

"I can't marry you, Lord Northampton," she started, hesitantly, "because I want to marry for love."

Everett bobbed his head. "As well as you should, which is why we aren't truly going to marry."

Now she was confused. "Pardon?" she asked, looking up at him.

He smiled at her. "We won't post the banns, but we will let it circulate that we have an understanding between us. By doing so, you will be allowed to have the Season you desire, with balls and soirées. I assure you that no one will reject you because of my name."

"But what happens at the end of the Season?"

"Come the end of the Season, we will mutually end our engagement, and I have no doubt that a long list of suitors will start vying for your attention, especially with a generous dowry of £30,000," he shared. "Then you will have the luxury of picking your own suitor."

Biting her lower lip, she asked, "What if I do not select a suitor?"

"Then I suppose you will have two options: marry me or reject me for another Season."

"And what of your reputation?"

"Men do not have the same restrictions as women do when it comes to their reputations," Everett replied, amused.

Without saying a word, Madalene rose and walked over to the window. Her eyes scanned the green hills. Did she dare take him up on his offer? What if it didn't work and the *ton* still ostracized her?

"Lady Madalene…" Everett started from behind her.

She turned back around to face him. "I would prefer it if we were not so formal."

"May I call you Maddie?"

"You may."

He smiled, and she noticed for the first time that he had a dimple in his right cheek. "Then you must call me Everett."

"I'd like that."

Everett's smile grew. "Are we in agreement then?"

Wrapping her arms around her waist, she asked, "Why are you doing this?"

His smiled dimmed. "It is not entirely unselfish, I assure you."

"Then why?"

His gaze shifted away from her. "I'm hounded by women and their scheming mothers wherever I go. By entering into this ruse with you, I won't have to constantly glance over my shoulder to ensure another young woman isn't trying to entrap me."

"Is it really that awful for you?"

He nodded. "Yes, I've even had young women sneak into my bedchamber. What's worse, they're encouraged by their own mothers to do so."

"Oh, that does sound awful," she murmured.

Everett stepped closer to her, and she breathed in his masculine scent of leather with a hint of orange. "I give you my word as a gentleman that I will protect you, Maddie."

His nearness was disconcerting, and her heart was beating rapidly. But then, she looked deep into his deep-set blue eyes, suddenly feeling calm and comforted. She trusted Everett. If he said this plan was going to work, then she was sure it would.

"I believe you," she said.

"Then you will be my betrothed," he paused, smiling flirtatiously, "until you break my heart by picking another suitor."

Motioning between them, she asked, "How will this work?"

"Well, I shall call upon you later, and we will take a carriage ride through Hyde Park during the fashionable hour. That should get the tongues wagging," he explained. "Then, this evening, we will attend the theatre with my mother."

"I do love the theatre." She smiled.

"It's important for us to be seen together to solidify the ruse, at least in the beginning."

Madalene nodded. "That sounds logical."

"Indeed." He reached for her ungloved hand and brought it to his lips. "Until tonight, my dear."

His lips lingered on her skin, causing her to lose all rational thought. Instead of responding, she just stared back at him.

He chuckled. "We'll need to work on your reaction to having your knuckles kissed."

Snatching back her hand, she huffed, "You just caught me off guard, that's all."

"Or is it because I am so incredibly charming?"

"That is most assuredly not the reason."

"Whatever you say, Maddie," he teased smugly.

A knock came at the door, and they each took a step back. The door opened, and Penelope and Nicholas entered.

"Are congratulations in order?" Nicholas asked.

Everett nodded. "Madalene has agreed to be my betrothed for the Season."

"That's wonderful news," Penelope murmured. "But we must hurry if we want to make our appointment at the modiste shop for your fitting."

"I will be just a moment as I fetch my gloves and reticule," Madalene said as she rushed out of the room.

She had the sudden urge to be alone. Oh my! What had she just agreed to?

6

Everett reined in his horse in front of his four-level townhouse. A footman rushed down the steps to relieve him of his horse.

His tall, balding butler opened the door for him and held out his hands for his gloves. “Welcome home, milord.”

“Thank you, Howe.” He glanced around the entry hall. “Is my mother home?”

“Yes, she’s in the drawing room.”

“Very good.”

Everett headed towards the drawing room, knowing this would be a rather awkward conversation. He would need to explain to his mother that he was engaged, but it was just a ruse to help the lovely Lady Madalene. And she was definitely lovely. Somehow, she had the uncanny ability to bewitch him at every encounter.

Stepping into the drawing room with its green-papered walls, he saw his mother sitting on the settee embroidering a white handkerchief.

“Morning, Mother.”

Lowering the handkerchief to her lap, she smiled at him, but her smile didn't reach her eyes. "Where did you run off to so early this morning?"

"I went to visit Nicholas," he said. At least that was the partial truth. His main purpose was to visit Lady Madalene and see how she was faring.

"To go riding?"

"We didn't ride today." He walked further into the room and sat down next to her. "Are you feeling all right?"

To his surprise, she shook her head. "Sadly, I'm not. I've been feeling increasingly weaker, and Dr. Grove says that my heart is starting to give out."

"When did the doctor come by?"

"This morning while you were out."

Everett reached out and embraced her. "We shall seek out the best doctors and cure you of all your ailments," he said in a firm but reassuring tone.

Leaning back, she gave him a tender smile. "You're a good son, but I'm getting older. This is what happens to old people."

"You're still young," he contended.

"Only in your eyes, my love." She brought her hand up to cup his cheek. "That's why lately I have been pushing you to find a bride. I want to see you settled, and possibly have a few grandchildren before I die."

Bollocks! He couldn't tell her the truth now… could he? No, he must.

He started off slowly as his mother lowered her hand. "Do you recall hearing about one of Isabella's friends from Miss Bell's Finishing School named Lady Madalene?"

"Yes, the one that loves to climb trees."

"Trees?"

She smiled. "She enjoys climbing trees almost as much as Isabella loves to go riding."

"Is that so?"

"It is," she revealed. "Have you not heard about Maddie's

antics at school from Isabella? Every time she comes home, she spends hours filling me in on what Maddie has said or done."

"I do not recall, but in my defense, Isabella rambles on and on." He smirked.

"That she does," his mother agreed, then gave him a quizzical look. "Why are you asking about Lady Madalene?"

"Well, it so happens that she jumped out of a tree and into my curricle yesterday as I was leaving Lord Powis's estate," he shared.

"Did she injure herself?"

"No, she didn't."

"Oh, good." His mother cocked her head. "What was she doing at Lord Powis's estate?"

"Apparently, the garden party was being hosted in her honor, and she was fleeing from her fiancé, Lord Tattershell."

"*She* is Lady Madalene Ramsbury?" She gasped.

"She is."

"That poor, poor dear," she sighed. "What a horrid man to be engaged to."

He shifted nervously in his seat. "She's not engaged to Lord Tattershell anymore."

"No?"

"Fortunately, Lady Madalene is close with the Duchess of Blackbourne, and I drove her straightaway to Hereford Hall. She is under the duke's protection now."

His mother's face softened. "That's wonderful news."

"It is." He rose and walked over to the mantel. "Her uncle, Lord Stafford, was forcing her into the marriage, and we believe he has some nefarious intentions towards her."

"Lord Stafford sounds like an awful man."

"He is," Everett mumbled.

His mother watched him curiously. "Are you feeling all right, my dear?"

"I am," he assured her as he picked up a small floral vase and fingered it. "This morning, Lord Stafford came to call on Lady Madalene and demanded that Nicholas turn the girl over to him."

"And did he?" his mother asked with wide, worried eyes.

"No." Everett shook his head. "But he was irate and accused me of ruining his niece."

"But that wasn't true, was it?"

Placing the vase down on the mantel, he replied, "It was not. Her reputation was ruined when she chose to flee the party. Luckily, no one has discovered that I drove her to Hereford Hall. If they had, I'm sure it would have been mentioned in the Society page."

"That poor girl," his mother muttered. "She was left with an impossible choice."

"True," he said, turning and leaning back against the mantel. "Which is why I offered for her."

His mother's mouth dropped open in surprise. "You what?"

"Given the circumstances, I felt it was best to…" His words stilled when his mother jumped up from the settee.

"What wonderful, unexpected news!" she exclaimed. "Lady Madalene is an excellent choice for your bride."

Everett held his hand up. "Wait, there is something I need to explain first." He hesitated for a moment. "Madalene has just turned eighteen, and I want to give her a Season first."

"That is most gracious of you," his mother said, practically dancing in excitement.

"At the end of the Season…"

She cut him off. "You shall post the banns and be married within three weeks' time."

"No, Mother," Everett placed his hand gently on her arm. "Not in three weeks. At the end of the Season…"

As if she hadn't heard, his mother clasped her hands in front of her. "I'm so proud of you, son. Not only did you help a young woman in need, but you chose a fine woman to be your marchioness."

"Mother, wait…"

She stared at him with a twinkle in her eye, something that had not been there when he had first walked in the room. How could he dash her new dreams of having Lady Madalene as her daughter-in-law?

"Yes?" she prodded.

Everett stifled a groan. He couldn't do it. He couldn't tell her the truth… at least, not yet. Instead, he said, "Madalene will be joining us for the theatre tonight."

"What delightful news! I cannot wait to meet her," his mother declared, approaching him. She cupped his right cheek, her eyes gleaming. "You have made me immensely happy, Everett."

He gave her a tentative smile. "I try."

Dropping her hand, she stepped back and maintained her smile. "I'm going to start sorting through the family jewels. I cannot wait to show Madalene the unique pieces. Perhaps she'll want to wear one to your engagement ball."

"Mother…"

She put her hand up and smiled. "Don't worry, son. I heard you. You aren't posting the banns until the end of the Season, but that doesn't mean we shouldn't start planning now for your engagement ball."

"I would prefer not to."

His mother laughed. "Dear heavens, why am I asking you? I'll ask Madalene when I see her tonight." Reaching down, she picked up her handkerchief off the table. "Thank you, Everett. I was sitting here wallowing in self-pity, and now I'm excited beyond words."

Everett slouched back against the mantel as he watched his mother depart from the room. What had he done? Somehow, he had the strength to stand up to Lord Stafford, but he didn't have the strength to disappoint his mother.

Eventually, she would discover the truth, and he prayed that it wouldn't kill her.

"Milord," his butler interrupted with a silver tray in his hands. "You have received a missive from His Grace, the Duke of Blackbourne."

"Bring it here," he ordered as he straightened.

Everett unfolded the note and read, "*Return to Hereford Hall. Immediately*." It wasn't addressed to him or even signed. Perhaps he needed to remind Nicholas how to write a missive.

He crumbled the note in his hand. "Prepare my curricle. Apparently, I am returning to Hereford Hall earlier than I had intended."

Stepping into Nicholas's study, Everett was surprised when his grace greeted him graciously.

"Excellent. You're here," the duke said.

"What was so important that you needed to see me right away?" Everett asked curiously.

Nicholas gestured towards a solemn-looking man sitting in an armchair with a drink in his hand, wearing a nondescript dark brown jacket. "Lord Northampton, allow me to introduce you to Mr. Percy Swinton. He's been assigned to us personally by Sir Nathaniel Conant, the Chief Magistrate of Bow Street."

"You're a Bow Street Runner?" Everett asked.

Mr. Swinton rose. "I am."

"I believe I made that rather clear," Nicholas muttered under his breath.

Ignoring his friend, Everett replied, "Thank you for coming so quickly, Mr. Swinton."

Mr. Swinton bowed. "You are welcome, milord. I happened

to be with Sir Nathaniel when his grace's missive arrived, and he asked me to take the case."

Nicholas came around his desk. "The case is rather straightforward. My wife's companion…"

"And my betrothed," Everett interjected.

"Yes, well," Nicholas continued, "her uncle, Lord Stafford, was forcing her into an unwanted marriage with Lord Tattershell."

Mr. Swinton's brows drew together. "Lord Tattershell is a most unsavory character."

"We're aware of that fact," Everett confirmed. "He arrived late to the garden party being held in his honor and was drunk in the bargain."

Placing his glass down on the drink cart, Mr. Swinton said, "That doesn't surprise me. He is a frequent visitor at the gambling halls across Town. The rumor is that he's gambled away his fortune."

"All of it?" Everett inquired.

"Yes, and then some," the Bow Street Runner confirmed.

"So, marrying an heiress would solve all his problems?" Nicholas questioned.

Mr. Swinton nodded. "Aye. That it would. Although, I'm sure he'd find a way to gamble away that money as well." He glanced between them. "But this girl somehow escaped her uncle's clutches?"

"Yes," Nicholas stated. "Lady Madalene was able to procure a ride with Lord Northampton, and he brought her straight here, where she is under my protection."

"That was a smart thing to do, your grace," Mr. Swinton acknowledged. "Lord Tattershell wouldn't dare cross you."

Picking up a paper from his desk, Nicholas said, "I'm afraid you're wrong there. Lord Tattershell is suing Lord Stafford, Lord Northampton, and myself for breach of contract."

"How did he file a lawsuit so quickly?" Everett asked as

Nicholas extended him the paper. He read the document, then shared, "He's asking for £50,000 as compensation."

Nicholas leaned back against his desk. "My solicitor has assured me that Lord Tattershell has no legal grounds to sue Lord Northampton or myself. He's just desperate enough to try anything."

"This lawsuit states that he will drop the matter if Lady Madalene agrees to marry him," Everett read.

"He's a cad. That doesn't surprise me that he would sink so low as to force a young woman's hand," Mr. Swinton stated. "Would you like me to keep tabs on Lord Tattershell?"

"Not at this time," Nicholas said. "Right now, we need your help in finding Mr. Simms. He was the late Earl Stafford's solicitor, and we believe he'll have a copy of the will."

"May I ask why you would like to see the will of the deceased earl?" the Bow Street Runner asked.

Everett laid the paper back on the desk. "Lord Stafford left his daughter a £30,000 dowry, but supposedly did not leave any other provisions for her."

"And you suspect that the current Lord Stafford is lying?" Mr. Swinton pressed.

"Yes," Everett and Nicholas said in unison.

Mr. Swinton sighed. "You must understand that wills can be destroyed or misplaced, especially if the heir does not want his predecessor's wishes known."

"We understand that," Nicholas acknowledged.

"Good," the Bow Street Runner said. "I shall consult with another Bow Street Runner, who may have the information we seek. With any luck, we shall locate Mr. Simms in short order and resolve this matter."

Everett walked over to the drink cart and took the lid off the decanter. "That would be most satisfactory," he said, pouring himself a drink.

"It shall be done then." Mr. Swinton bowed and departed from the room.

Coming around his desk, Nicholas sat down in the chair. "How did your mother take the news about the feigned engagement."

Everett hung his head. "I couldn't tell her."

"You *what*?"

"I couldn't tell her," he repeated, bringing his gaze back up. "She told me how proud she was of me for saving Lady Madalene and doing the right thing by offering for her."

To his great annoyance, Nicholas started laughing, loudly. "What a tangled web of deceit you have created for yourself. Your mother will eventually discover the truth when the Season ends, and you don't post the banns."

"Thank you for the reminder," Everett growled.

Nicholas's smile grew. "I should not delight in your misery, but I do."

Everett sipped his drink, then attempted to change topics. "Where is your mother?"

"She's spending time at our country estate, but she should be arriving in a fortnight," Nicholas shared.

"Ah, that makes sense," he said, placing the glass down onto the drink cart. "Now if you will excuse me, I am going to take Madalene on a carriage ride through Hyde Park."

"Enjoy the fashionable hour," Nicholas said, reaching for a ledger. "I have work to do."

7

Madalene anxiously stared out of the drawing room window. She was waiting for Lord Northampton… er… Everett to call on her. A straw bonnet sat atop her head, and nervously she tied and untied the bonnet strings as she waited.

Penelope's voice broke through her musings. "You look nervous, Maddie."

Turning away from the window, she admitted, "I am. Dreadfully so."

"May I ask why?"

Taking a deep breath, Madalene tied the bonnet strings firmly under her chin. "How am I supposed to act around a man that is pretending to be my fiancé?"

"Just be your charming self."

Madalene huffed. "Now you are being ridiculous."

"You're overthinking this," Penelope contended. "This ruse is meant to help both of you."

"Good point," she replied, although a bit reluctantly.

"Besides, what's the worst thing that could happen?"

Madalene pressed her lips together. "Everett would be forced to marry me."

"Would that be so bad?" Penelope asked. "He is a marquess, and a handsome one at that."

Walking over to the settee, Madalene dropped down onto it in a most unladylike fashion. "I suppose I wanted the chance to marry for love, like you did."

"Then seize this opportunity. Everett was right about one thing. By the end of the Season, you will have suitors vying for your attention," Penelope encouraged.

"What gentleman would be interested in a woman who has an understanding with another man?"

Her friend grinned. "You clearly do not understand the ways of men."

"Regardless, who would want to court me, Penelope?" Madalene asked in earnest. "I'm a socially inept girl, barely out of the school room. To make matters worse, I already have a tattered reputation."

Compassion filled the duchess's eyes. "You are much too hard on yourself. That's how you see yourself, but that's not how the world sees you." She walked over and sat down next to her. "I find you to be a kind, remarkable young woman that used to make me giggle in class with your antics."

"Thank you," Madalene murmured. "I've struggled to find myself in this world since my parents died. I feel inferior to others in so many ways."

"It's easy to compare yourself to others, but that only hurts *you* in the end. You must understand that there is not a person in the whole world who thinks and acts like you do. Not one."

Madalene laughed. "I daresay that's a good thing. My thoughts can be quite jumbled."

"You can confide in Everett about your worries," Penelope said. "He's a good man, and he'll help you navigate through these treacherous waters."

"Treacherous waters?"

Penelope smirked. "That's what it is like dealing with the

ton. They are a bunch of busybodies and will pounce on you the moment they see any sign of weakness."

"That sounds horrifying."

"It is," the duchess confirmed. "But it's all a game; a game that *you* can win."

Madalene sat on the edge of her seat. "How?"

"I cannot tell you that," Penelope asserted. "Every game has different players, different rules. You must plan your course of action accordingly."

A man chuckled from the doorway. "You're being rather intense, Penelope."

"I think I'm being rather practical. After all, I have personally experienced the highs and lows of Society," Penelope responded.

"That is a true statement," Everett remarked, walking further into the room. "But now the *ton* falls at your feet, your grace." He bowed.

Penelope rose from the settee. "Save your flowery, insincere words for someone more gullible than I, Everett."

"You wound me," he teased, dramatically placing a hand over his heart.

"I doubt that," Penelope bantered. "Well, if you will excuse me, I plan to coax Nicholas away from his ledgers by suggesting we go riding through Hyde Park."

After Penelope exited the room, Everett turned his attention towards her and smiled kindly. "Are you ready for a carriage ride, my lady?"

"I am." She rose and approached him.

Everett offered his arm as his eyes perused the length of her. "You are looking beautiful this fine afternoon, Maddie."

A blush crept up her cheeks as she placed her hand in the crook of his arm. "Thank you, Everett."

"I must admit I enjoy hearing my name on your lips," he murmured, leading her towards the entry hall.

Dear heavens, he was flirting with her! How was she to respond? Quick, think of something, she told herself. She seemed to remember from finishing school that girls talked about batting their eyelashes at gentlemen.

She batted her eyelashes at Everett. "I like when you say my name, as well." There. That should do.

He looked at her curiously. "Did you just attempt to flirt with me?" he asked, amusement in his tone.

"No, I was just attempting to make conversation," she hurried to say as embarrassment washed over her.

The butler opened the door, and Everett cast her a knowing look as he led her down the stairs.

Stopping in front of the curricle, he stated, "I saw you bat your eyelashes at me."

"I was just blinking," she lied. "I had something in my eye."

Everett laughed as he assisted her into the curricle. "You are a horrible liar, my dear."

Realizing lying was futile, she admitted, "All right. I was attempting to flirt with you."

"For what purpose?"

Madalene lowered her voice. "I have never flirted with a man before."

"That was painfully obvious."

She shifted to face him. "Will you teach me?"

"You want me to teach you how to flirt with a man?" he asked in disbelief.

"Yes."

He smirked. "But I only know how to flirt with women."

"You're insufferable," she declared.

Everett laughed again as he walked to the other side of the curricle and sat down next to her on the bench. He reached for the reins and urged the team forward.

Pursing her lips, she admonished, "Will you please refrain from laughing *at* me?"

His smiled dimmed, but it didn't entirely go away. "I promise that I am not laughing at you."

"Then why are you laughing?"

"I don't know why, but I find you quite amusing."

"Well, stop it."

He arched an eyebrow. "Stop finding you amusing?"

She tensed. "No, stop laughing at me whenever you twist our conversation around."

"I can't promise that."

Turning her gaze towards the pavement, she was content to ignore her pretend fiancé during their carriage ride. Men, women, and children lined the pavement as they rushed about, skirting around the street sellers hawking their wares against the buildings.

"I can only speak for myself, but I prefer when a woman is forthright and honest," Everett shared, breaking the silence. "I would rather have a young woman speak her mind than try to say only what she thinks I want to hear. Furthermore, I detest coquettes."

Madalene turned her gaze back towards him. "I thought men wanted to be told how dashingly handsome they are."

"You are always welcome to express how handsome I am, using as many words as possible," he said in a teasing tone.

She found herself returning his smile. "You're incorrigible."

"Ah, incorrigible is better than insufferable," he stated victoriously. "I'm winning you over with my witty banter."

Wringing her hands in her lap, she admitted, "I just turned eighteen, and I feel socially inadequate when it comes to mingling with gentlemen."

"I think you're doing just fine."

"You do?"

Everett nodded encouragingly. "Indeed. I have been thoroughly enjoying our outing."

"You have?" she asked, lifting her brow.

Turning his attention back towards the street, he said, "Don't tell Penelope, but I disagree with her."

"In what way?"

"You don't need to come up with a battleplan to deal with the ton, rather *we* need to come up with a battleplan."

"*We*?"

Everett nudged her shoulder with his. "We're a team. At least for now. We'll navigate those treacherous waters… together."

"How long were you standing there?"

"Long enough," he admitted. "You can trust me, Maddie."

"I do trust you, Everett."

He smiled an achingly sweet smile that caused her breath to hitch. Good heavens! She needed to stop acting like a simpering debutante. This was not a real engagement.

As he directed the team into Hyde Park, he said, "I understand you like to climb trees, and apparently, not just to escape despicable fiancés."

"Where did you hear that?" she asked cautiously.

"My mother told me, but she got her information from Isabella," he replied as their shoulders brushed up against each other. "But I'm curious. Is it true?"

Everett watched as a bright smile came to Madalene's face, transforming her entire expression. If her goal was to charm, she did so beautifully. Yet, he did not believe this was an act. She was too innocent, too sweet. She was nothing like the other women of the *ton*.

"Oh, I do love climbing trees," she admitted in a low, conspiring voice. "But you must not tell another soul."

"That's an interesting pastime."

Her eyes scanned the trees along the road. "My father studied birds and spent his days cataloging the various species surrounding our country estate, Mowbray Hall, in South Benfleet." She sighed. "From a young age, I recall climbing trees and remaining perfectly still as he sketched the birds. It was wonderful."

Everett cast her a look of disbelief. "Your idea of fun is to spend hours in a tree, while being as quiet as possible?"

"It is."

"You and I certainly have different definitions of fun." He chuckled.

She brought her gaze back to his. "Whenever I climb a tree, it reminds me of my father and the hours we used to spend together."

"Did your mother ever join you?"

Madalene nodded. "She would never climb the trees, mind you, but she would bring along a picnic and a book. She would sit under the shade of the tree and read until it was time to break for a meal."

Curiosity overcame his sense of propriety, and he found himself asking, "How did your parents die?"

Her voice grew tight. "Typhoid fever. They died within days of each other."

"I am sorry for your loss," he murmured, his eyes remaining straight ahead. His words felt wholly inadequate to his ears.

"Thank you. It hasn't even been a year yet." He could hear the anguish in her voice.

Glancing at her white gown, he wondered why she wasn't in mourning clothes, but he felt he'd already pushed the bounds of polite conversation where this topic was concerned.

As if she could read his thoughts, she said, "You must be wondering why I am not wearing mourning clothes."

"I was."

She started fingering the strings to her bonnet. "My uncle demanded I wear more lively colors when he summoned me from Miss Bell's. He stated that I had mourned my parents long enough."

"That's awful," Everett expressed.

"One can never truly prepare for the loss and grief of losing their parents, but I found comfort in the arms of my friends at school. They became my family."

He gave her a weak smile. "I am happy that you were not alone during that time."

"Your sister, Isabella, was a source of great support to me," she said.

Mulling over her words in silence, he almost missed her next question.

"What was your childhood like?"

"You and I had vastly different childhoods," he shared. "My brothers, sister, and I ran my parents ragged with our mischievousness."

"Is that so?"

He chuckled as they started to ride parallel to the Serpentine River. "We spent our summers outside, playing in the woods, and making entirely too much noise to keep any birds perched in our trees. On more than one occasion, we attempted to craft boats, but they always sank to the bottom of the pond near our estate."

"How many did you attempt to make?"

"About ten."

Madalene giggled. "At least you were persistent."

"That we were," he responded, grinning.

With mirth in her eyes, she suggested, "Perhaps on our next outing we can climb trees."

"I don't mean to brag, but I'm rather proficient at tree climbing," he declared, puffing out his chest with exaggerated pride.

Madalene smiled. "Is that so?"

"It is," he confirmed. "My brothers and I spent hours climbing trees every day, much to my parents' dismay."

"And what of Isabella?"

Everett shrugged. "Frankly, I don't know. She's eleven years my junior. When I left for Eton at thirteen, she was still in the nursery."

"Did you not come home on holiday?"

"I did, but my father preferred me to spend as much time as possible at school, first Eton, then Oxford. He said it was my duty as the heir to receive the best possible education."

"What of your brothers?"

"One is an officer in His Majesty's Royal Navy, and the other one is a barrister," he replied, attempting to keep the bitterness out of his tone. "It's exactly how my father envisioned our futures."

Madalene placed her hand on his sleeve. "You don't seem pleased by their choice of professions."

Adjusting the reins in his hand, he felt increasingly uncomfortable with her line of questioning. "I'm not," he muttered, hoping she would take the hint and leave him be.

To his surprise, she said, "Well, if your brothers turned out to be even half the man that you are, then they would be most fortunate."

"Why would you say that?" he asked, turning to face her.

The kindness in her eyes was unmistakable. "You're an honorable gentleman. You are my hero."

"No," he said with a shake of his head. "You saved yourself. You ran away, climbed a tree, and jumped into my curricle."

"True, but you could have returned me to the party. Or ordered me out of the curricle."

A flirtatious smile grew on his face. "I would never have done that to a woman as beautiful as you."

Rather than blush as he expected, Madalene shook her head lightly. "I fear that I'm growing immune to your charms, my lord."

Impossible. "I shall have to work harder to earn your affection then."

"I'm excited to go to the theatre tonight," she remarked, changing the subject. "Penelope informed me that Miss Rose Stephen is performing tonight at Covent Gardens. I have longed to hear her soprano voice."

Everett reached up and adjusted his cravat. It was time for him to confess that he hadn't been entirely honest with his mother.

"About that..." he started slowly, "when I started to tell my Mother about us..." His voice stopped as Madalene lifted her brow expectedly.

"Yes... Everett," she prodded.

"When I told my mother about our engagement, she was overjoyed, and I didn't have the heart to tell her the truth." He held his breath, waiting for her response.

"Oh," she replied. "Do you think that's wise?"

He shook his head. "No, but my mother informed me that her heart is growing increasingly weaker, and she only wants me to be happily settled down."

Madalene shifted to face him. "That's rather cruel, don't you think? Giving your mother false hope?"

Wincing, he agreed, "I know."

"When do you plan to tell her the truth?"

"Soon," he responded. "But until then, we will need to pretend to be smitten with each other around my mother."

"Smitten?"

A flirtatious smile came to his lips. "Would you prefer enamored or besotted with?"

"I suppose I can appear smitten with you, but it will take much effort on my part," she said dramatically.

"Is that so?"

She nodded. "You may not be aware of this fact, but you are rather an unlikable chap."

"Chap?"

With a twinkle of mischief in her eyes, she replied, "I promise that your secret is safe with me, my lord."

"No more 'my lord' for you," he chided lightly. "We are engaged to be married."

"We are pretending to be engaged," she corrected.

"That's what I meant." He looked at her curiously. "Do you intend to tell Isabella the truth?"

Madalene shook her head. "I had planned to write her after the Season concluded."

"Perhaps it might be best if you wrote and told her the truth now."

"Do you think that's wise, especially since your mother doesn't know?"

"I do."

Unexpectedly, Madalene gasped as she pointed towards the trees. "Do you see the Red Kite in the beech tree?"

Following her hand, he saw an elegant bird with red and white feathers perched high above them.

"In 1758, Carl Linnaeus described the Red Kite in the tenth edition of his *Systema Naturae*," Madalene shared.

"That is… fascinating."

She laughed. "Liar."

"I must admit that bird watching does not excite me," he said.

"Then what does?"

He paused. Madalene's question caught him off guard. What did excite him? For so long, he had been going through the motions. Did anything excite him anymore?

"Come, we must get you home to change for the theatre," he said, watching her as her eyes hungrily scoured the trees looking for birds.

One thing he knew for sure, he would never tire of Madalene's enthusiasm and goodness.

8

Wearing a black jacket, white waistcoat with matching cravat, and dark trousers, Everett waited for Madalene at the bottom of the stairs in the entry of Hereford Hall, trying to ignore his friend's vain attempts to threaten him.

"If you touch her, I will kill you," Nicholas growled.

Everett smirked. "Pray tell, how exactly would you kill me?"

"There are so many options afforded to me that I'm afraid I couldn't pick just one right now."

"But if you had to?" he pressed.

Nicholas seemed to mull over his response. "I suppose I would draw and quarter you."

"That's an interesting choice, your grace, but you need not fret," Everett assured him. "My mother is in the coach, so we will be properly chaperoned."

"I'm warning you…"

Everett cut him off. "Aren't you being overly protective of my betrothed?"

Nicholas gave him an exasperated look. "You aren't truly engaged. You do know that, right?"

"It was just a slip of the tongue," he replied. Why did he

continue to make that same mistake? Of course he knew this was just a ruse.

Glancing up, he saw that Madalene had begun descending the stairs with Penelope by her side. He stood transfixed; his mouth opened at the sight of her. Her hair was piled high on top of her head and had pearls entwined. Her white dress hugged her curves perfectly. She was a vision of perfection.

Nicholas leaned over and quipped, "Your mouth is still open."

Everett quickly closed his mouth as Madalene came to stand in front of him.

"You look breathtaking, Maddie," he said, his eyes roaming her face.

She smiled up at him. "Thank you, Everett. You look rather handsome yourself."

"Are you flirting with me?" He smiled.

"No. I'm just stating a fact."

"Then by all means, please state away."

Nicholas grunted, "Remember Everett…" His voice trailed off.

"I will remember, your grace."

Everett offered his arm to Madalene, whisking her out of Hereford Hall and into the awaiting coach. As he assisted her into the coach, he smelled the delightful aroma of rosewater in her hair.

He climbed in after her and sat next to his mother as the coach jerked forward.

Not one to waste a moment, Lady Northampton smiled tenderly at Madalene. "You are exquisite, just as I imagined you would be."

"Thank you, Lady Northampton," Madalene murmured respectfully.

His mother shook her head. "You must call me Mary. After all, we are practically family."

"That is most gracious of you," Madalene acknowledged. "Then I must insist that you call me Madalene."

Mary nodded in approval. "I am delighted to meet you, my dear child. Isabella has shared so many stories about your days at finishing school that I feel as if I already know you."

Madalene's eyes nervously darted towards her. "May I ask what stories she shared?"

"For starters, I know that you love climbing trees, are fluent in multiple languages, excel at the pianoforte, and that Isabella complains constantly that you compel her to brush up on her needlework," his mother listed.

Everett saw Madalene visibly relax.

"Isabella would much rather be riding her horse than practicing embroidery," she responded.

"Yes, sadly, that has always been the case," Lady Northampton replied. "When she was younger, her governess used to teach her lessons while she sat atop her horse."

Madalene giggled, and she tossed her gloved hand up to cover her lips. "That sounds like Isabella."

Growing solemn, Mary said, "I'm so glad that you had the courage to run away from Lord Tattershell. You are quite a brave young lady."

"Thank you," Madalene replied gratefully. "No one has ever called me brave before."

Everett interjected, "I believe I hinted at it earlier."

"Well, you are," Lady Northampton assured her. "And I am overjoyed that you have accepted my son's suit. I never thought he would settle down, much less with a kind, virtuous woman such as yourself."

"Mother…" Everett warned.

Waving her hand dismissively in front of her, his mother pressed on. "I can tell that you will make Everett happy, and that is all that I have ever wanted for him."

Madalene pressed her lips together, looking as if she might

cry. "You should know, your son is a true gentleman. He saved me that day, and he continues to save me every day with the love and kindness that he bestows upon me."

Tears came to Mary's eyes. "You are a godsend, my child."

Everett shot Madalene a pointed look, and she surprised him by winking back. Good heavens, he thought, she could have a career in theatre.

The coach came to a stop, and a footman opened the door. Everett exited and turned to assist his mother out of the coach. When it came time to assist Madalene, he waited till she stepped onto the ground before he leaned in and whispered, "Well played, Maddie."

She tilted her face towards him. "Never underestimate me, Everett. I can be quite useful."

"I have no doubt," he replied, his eyes lingering on her lips.

His mother cleared her throat. "Son, there is a line of carriages waiting."

As he escorted them into the theatre, Everett felt incredible pride that Madalene was on his right arm. Nearly every man and woman in the hall stopped and stared at Madalene as she walked by. She seemed to have no awareness of the stir she was creating amongst the *ton*.

A familiar man broke through the crowd and approached them. Baldwin, the Viscount of Mountgarret, extended his arm towards Everett. "I understand congratulations are in order," he remarked jovially.

Everett shook his hand. "They are. But how did you hear so soon?"

Baldwin chuckled. "Apparently, you took a ride through Hyde Park with your betrothed during the fashionable hour."

"Ah, that makes sense." Everett gestured towards Madalene. "Lord Mountgarret, allow me to introduce you to my betrothed, Lady Madalene Ramsbury."

Mountgarret bowed. "It's a pleasure to meet you, Lady Madalene."

"Likewise, Lord Mountgarret," Madalene replied and curtseyed respectfully.

"Lord Mountgarret is Penelope's cousin," Everett informed her. "And at one point, he was Nicholas's arch-enemy."

Madalene smiled. "Is that so?"

Lord Mountgarret nodded. "It's true. His grace was under the impression that I had nefarious intentions when it came to my cousin."

"Oh dear," Madalene muttered.

"That's in the past now, and I consider Nicholas to be a dear friend." Lord Mountgarret glanced over his shoulder in a panic. "But don't tell him I said that." He winked at her to indicate he was joking.

Everett didn't like the way Baldwin was looking at Madalene, and he placed his hand on the small of her back. "Are you attending the theatre alone tonight?"

"I came with friends," Baldwin said, his eyes lingering on Madalene.

"If you will excuse us, we must find our box before the show starts," Everett said as he began leading Madalene away.

Why did the thought of Baldwin flirting with Madalene cause him to have the sudden urge to challenge his friend to a duel? He was being ridiculous. This is what he wanted for Madalene; to have a long list of gentlemen vying for her attention. Right?

Upon arrival at their private box, he was pleased when his mother indicated they should sit in the front two seats. Madalene sat down and leaned to look over the edge.

"How many people are down in the gallery?" she asked.

"I would imagine about eight hundred," he answered. "It only costs two shillings to be in the gallery."

"Extraordinary," she murmured.

Keeping his eyes fixed on her, he said, "It is."

She tilted her head up and admired the elegant chandeliers. "What a lovely theatre."

"Have you never been to Covent Gardens before, Madalene?" his mother asked from behind them.

"No, my lady," she answered. "This is my first visit."

"You are in for a treat then," Lady Northampton said. "Miss Rose Stephen is spectacular."

Shifting in her chair, Madalene replied, "Isabella told me as much. She said her voice is angelic."

"It's true," his mother agreed, her eyes roaming the stage. "You should know that this theatre has an interesting history. It was destroyed by fire in 1808 and was reopened in 1809, just ten months after Prince George laid the cornerstone for the new theatre."

Everett joined the conversation. "In a desperate attempt to recover some of the costs of rebuilding, the theatre management increased the ticket prices, causing the audience to loudly protest during the opening performance of *Macbeth*."

"What did the management do in response?" Madalene asked.

"They had no choice but to reduce the ticket price. The disruptions lasted for nearly two months," he informed her.

"Two months?"

A hush fell over the crowd as a man walked onto the stage. For the next short while, Everett just sat back and watched Madalene's glistening eyes as she took in the opera. She seemed to be entranced, and her excitement fairly radiated off her person. How does someone find so much joy in a mere opera, he wondered.

When the intermission was announced, he saw Madalene jump up from her seat and start clapping. "That was exhilarating," she proclaimed in a cheerful voice. "I can't wait for the second half."

His mother rose. "Everett, would you mind seeking out some refreshment for us?"

"I would be honored." He took a step closer to Madalene and whispered in her ear, "I shall be right back. Will you miss me?"

"Does a person miss a thorn in their boot?" she countered, holding back a smile.

He chuckled at her attempt to insult him. "I shall be back shortly."

The moment the door was closed, Lady Northampton turned towards Madalene and said, "Now that Everett is gone, let's have ourselves a little chat, shall we?" She patted the seat next to her.

"What would you like to discuss?" Madalene asked warily as she sat down.

Lady Northampton smiled. "Why don't we start with what is really going on between you and my son?"

"Whatever do you mean?" she questioned, attempting to keep her voice calm.

"Well, this is supposed to be a marriage of convenience, but you two appear rather fond of each other."

Madalene gripped the sides of the chair. "I *am* fond of your son."

"After only two days?"

Tilting her chin almost defiantly, she replied, "He did rescue me from a rather unfortunate situation."

"Indeed," Lady Northampton said, her critical eye sweeping over her son's fiancée. "Perhaps it might be best if I go first."

"By all means," she encouraged.

Removing the fan from around her wrist, Lady Northampton started fanning her face. "I believe that you two concocted an engagement. But for what purpose, I am not sure."

"Why would you say that?"

"It's simple," Lady Northampton replied. "My son was tiring of the marriage mart, and you were a damsel that needed rescuing. My only question is, do you actually intend to marry my son?"

Pressing her lips together, Madalene turned her gaze back towards the stage. Did she dare boldly lie to Everett's mother?

"It's all right, child," Lady Northampton said, patting her knee with her fan. "Your secret will be safe with me."

Madalene turned her gaze back towards Lady Northampton. "My uncle was determined that I was to marry Lord Tattershell, so Everett stepped up and offered for me."

"That was most kind of him."

"It was," she admitted. "But at first, I turned him down."

"I see."

Wincing, she shared, "A few of the other girls at Miss Bell's Finishing School vowed to only marry for love, and Isabella and I made a similar promise to each other. When I explained that to Everett, he informed me that he had no intention of marrying me, but he wanted to give me a Season."

Lady Northampton's brows lifted. "Your intention is to break the engagement at the end of the Season."

"It is."

Lady Northampton laid the fan on her lap. "Don't you worry about your reputation?"

"Everett is insistent that I will have suitors vying for my attention come the end of the Season when we break the engagement."

"Did he state why?"

She nodded. "Because of my £30,000 dowry."

"That's an impressive dowry," Lady Northampton said. "And my son is encouraging you to meet other gentleman?"

"He is."

"Interesting. Then, I wonder why Everett was grinding his

teeth when Viscount Mountgarret was speaking to you?"

Madalene gave her a baffled look. "You must be mistaken. Everett has no designs on me."

"I know what I saw," Lady Northampton said with a smile.

"Regardless, Everett saved me from my uncle, and I saved him from the marriage mart. It is an alliance of sorts."

"At least until next Season," Everett's mother corrected.

The unpleasant thought of Everett marrying another came into her mind, and she averted her gaze from Lady Northampton.

"Do you care for my son?"

Madalene looked up. "I do, but not in the way you're implying."

"I see."

"What do you see?"

"Nothing, my dear." Lady Northampton smirked.

Before she could ask another question, a knock came at the door.

"I shall answer that. No doubt it is one of your admirers," Lady Northampton said as she walked towards the door.

As she opened the door, Lord Tattershell came barging into the room and approached Madalene.

"What is the meaning of this?" Lady Northampton asked from behind him.

"Nothing to concern yourself about, milady," Lord Tattershell remarked dismissively over his shoulder. "I just wanted a chance to speak to my fiancée."

Madalene rose from her seat and faced him. "We are not engaged anymore."

"We are," Lord Tattershell stated. "Your uncle gave you to me."

"I belong to no one," she said defiantly.

He took a commanding step closer to her. "You would break our engagement just because we got off on the wrong foot…"

"You were drunk and called me the wrong name… multiple

times," she huffed.

The anger in his eyes dissipated somewhat. "And I will spend the rest of our lives apologizing for our unfortunate first encounter."

Madalene shook her head. "I will not marry you."

"Is it because I am only a lowly viscount, and you have managed to catch yourself a marquess?"

Madalene gasped. "How dare you presume I am only interested in Lord Northampton because of his title?"

His eyes narrowed. "What exactly am I to presume? You were engaged to me one day, and the following day you were engaged to another."

"That is of your own doing," she challenged.

"No," he scoffed. "Do you want to know what I think?"

"I do not care to know…"

He cut her off. "You had no intention of marrying me."

Madalene pursed her lips, not knowing what to say. He spoke the truth.

"Well, Lady Madalene, I still intend to marry you," he said, leaning closer and lowering his voice. "And when you take another ride through Hyde Park, I will be there, watching you make a fool of yourself with Lord Northampton."

She swallowed nervously. "You followed me? Why would you do such a thing?"

"Because you are mine," he said as she felt his foul breath on her cheek.

Lady Northampton spoke up, her voice firm and unyielding. "It's time for you to go, sir, or I shall seek out the guards."

"I agree," he stated, straightening up, his eyes unwavering. "But I promise that this is not a goodbye, my pet."

Madalene tensed at his term of affection. "You need to leave."

His eyes traveled lewdly down the length of her body. "You look beautiful tonight." He turned towards Lady Northampton and bowed. "Thank you for allowing me to speak to my Madalene."

"Lady Madalene is engaged to my son, Lord Northampton," she declared haughtily.

"We shall see," Lord Tattershell responded before turning to leave the room.

Madalene collapsed onto the chair and took a deep breath.

"I presume that was Lord Tattershell." Lady Northampton sat down next to her.

"It was," she admitted. "Did you hear what he said to me?"

"Not all of it."

Clenching her fists in her lap, Madalene confessed, "He said that I belonged to him."

"That's absurd."

The door was pushed open, revealing Everett with a tray of macaroons, dried fruits, and comfits. "I wasn't sure what sounded appetizing, so I brought a sampling of the desserts being sold downstairs." His smile faded as his eyes darted between them. "What's wrong?"

"Lord Tattershell came to call on Madalene," his mother revealed.

After placing the tray on a side table in the back, Everett rushed and knelt in front of her. "What did he say?"

"He threatened me," she confessed. "He said that I belonged to him, and that he won't let me go."

Immediately, she found herself wrapped up in Everett's comforting arms. "I won't let anything happen to you, Maddie," he said firmly. "I will keep you safe."

She found herself relaxing into his embrace, finding solace. "He scared me, Everett. He told me that he followed us to Hyde Park."

"He did?"

"Yes, and he said he watched me make a fool of myself with you."

"Don't concern yourself with him. He's just angry," he whispered into her hair.

She shuddered. "I'm frightened."

Leaning back, Everett placed his hand on her right cheek. "No harm will come to you, I promise."

"Thank you," she murmured.

"Come, I think we should take you home," he suggested, rising.

She nodded and stood. "I think that would be for the best."

"I've been told that I am rather clever," he joked, but she did not miss the anger in his voice.

Accepting his proffered arm, Madalene stayed close to Everett as he led them towards their coach. She remained quiet as her eyes darted around the theatre, looking for any sign of Lord Tattershell. As she was about to step into the coach, she saw him step out of the shadows of the theatre. He tipped his hat at her.

Madalene froze on the pavement.

"What's wrong, Maddie?" Everett asked, squeezing her hand.

"Lord Tattershell," she managed to whisper.

Everett turned his gaze towards the direction she was staring, but Lord Tattershell had already disappeared back into the shadows. "Where?"

"He was right there."

"It's all right. He can't harm you," he encouraged.

Madalene stepped into the carriage and sat across from Lady Northampton. To her surprise, and great relief, Everett sat next to her and reached for her gloved hand.

"It will be all right," he assured her.

Madalene had expected his mother to issue a rebuke for Everett's show of affection, but she just nodded approvingly. Madalene smiled tentatively, grateful for Lady Northampton's support. Having Everett near her provided her with a great deal of comfort.

9

Riding in his plush coach, Everett leaned his head back and closed his eyes. Last night, after he'd escorted Madalene back to Hereford Hall, he had tossed and turned all night. She had barely said a word the whole drive back, and he was furious that Lord Tattershell had treated her so horribly. He would make certain that Lord Tattershell never spoke to Madalene again.

Nicholas had sent over a missive earlier this morning to inform him that Mr. Swinton had contacted him. The Bow Street Runner wanted to meet with them before breakfast.

The coach came to a stop in front of Hereford Hall. He stepped down and jogged up the few stairs.

The door opened before he had a chance to knock, and the butler greeted him. "Morning, Lord Northampton."

"Morning, Hawkins. Where is the duke?"

"In his study, milord." The butler closed the door behind him. "Would you like me to announce you?"

"No, thank you," Everett replied, walking across the marble entry. He stopped and spun around. "Has Lady Madalene come down for breakfast yet?"

"She has not."

"Excellent," he mumbled. "Will you inform me when she arrives for breakfast?"

Hawkins tipped his head. "As you wish."

Turning back on his heel, he walked over to Nicholas's study and flung open the door.

"Blazes, Everett," Nicholas declared, jumping up from his seat. "Whatever is the matter with you?"

Before answering, Everett stepped over to the drink cart. "I had a fitful night."

"Apparently."

He poured himself a brandy. "When is Mr. Swinton arriving?"

"Any minute now." Nicholas frowned. "It's rather early to be drinking."

Gripping the snifter in his hand, Everett admitted, "I just can't get that look of fear in Madalene's eyes out of my head."

"We'll keep her safe," Nicholas attempted to assure him.

Everett brought the snifter up to his lips. "Like I did last night?"

"What exactly happened last night?"

Lowering his glass, he stared at the brown liquid in the bottom and sighed. "While I was getting refreshments for the ladies, Lord Tattershell visited our box and harassed Madalene. He claimed that she belonged to him."

"That's awful."

"He frightened the poor girl. I never thought he might approach her in such a public place." Everett downed the last swallow, then placed his empty snifter back on the drink cart. He dropped down on the nearby camelback settee.

"Why would you?"

Before he could reply, a knock came at the door, and Hawkins announced, "Mr. Swinton is here to see you, your grace."

"Send him in," Nicholas ordered with a flick of his wrist.

Mr. Swinton walked into the room with a file in his hand. He stopped and bowed. "Morning, your grace, Lord Northampton."

"Morning," they both mumbled.

"I have some rather alarming news," Mr. Swinton declared as he sat in a chair across from Everett.

"More alarming than my fiancée being accosted by Lord Tattershell at Covent Gardens last night?" Everett growled.

"My apologies, milord," Mr. Swinton said, adjusting his jacket. "But the Bow Street Runner trailing Lord Tattershell did not want to give away his advantage."

Everett jumped to his feet. "His advantage?"

"Lady Madalene was in no danger of being assaulted or my man would have stepped in," Mr. Swinton asserted.

"Tattershell harassed my fiancée!" Everett shouted. "He should have been arrested."

Mr. Swinton met his gaze, unflinchingly. "We cannot arrest a man for visiting Covent Gardens and speaking to a lady."

"Mr. Swinton is right, Everett," Nicholas said.

"What is the point of having a man trail Lord Tattershell if he didn't even make his presence known last night?" Everett asked.

"We did not want to lose our advantage," Mr. Swinton repeated.

Huffing loudly, Everett sat back down on the settee. "That is inconceivable to me."

"I do have rather some unfortunate news to share," Mr. Swinton said, reaching for the file next to him. "Mr. Simms is dead."

"When?" Nicholas asked.

"That's the ticklish part," the Bow Street Runner stated. "He was found dead the day before Lord and Lady Stafford's funeral."

Leaning forward in his seat, Everett inquired, "How did he die?"

"He was floating face up in the River Thames," Mr. Swinton

revealed, opening the file. "There were no leads, no suspects, and no motive. The case was closed shortly thereafter, and it was ruled as an accidental death."

Nicholas walked over and sat next to Everett. "An accidental death?" he questioned.

Mr. Swinton frowned. "Men and women drown all the time in the River Thames. We don't have the resources to investigate each death."

"Do you believe that Lord Stafford had something to do with Mr. Simms's death?" Everett inquired.

"It's too early to determine that. However, I have reopened the case and assigned a man to start investigating his death," Mr. Swinton shared. "It just seems too great of a coincidence to dismiss it entirely.

"Good," Nicholas murmured.

Mr. Swinton removed a paper from the file. "This is a list of debts that Lord Stafford has accrued in various London gambling dens."

Accepting the paper, Everett's eyes scanned the long list. "How far is he in debt?"

"Approximately, £20,000."

Nicholas let out a low whistle. "That is a large sum."

"It is," the Bow Street Runner confirmed. "Lord Stafford had been banned from the gambling dens for lack of funds, but recently he was welcomed back with open arms. Would you like to guess when that was?"

"Pray tell," Nicholas said.

"It was the day of the garden party," Mr. Swinton stated.

Everett's brows lifted. "That can't be a coincidence."

"In my line of work, there is no such thing as a coincidence."

Rising, Everett walked over to the window and looked out. "That's not logical. If Madalene married Lord Tattershell, Stafford would have had to pay out £30,000 for her dowry."

"Correct, but somehow Stafford is benefiting from her marriage," Nicholas pointed out. "But how?"

Mr. Swinton closed the file in his hands. "Without Mr. Simms, we have no proof that a will even existed, other than Lord Stafford's word."

"If that was the case, then why did Lord Stafford even give his niece such a large dowry?" Everett asked.

"A dowry can be set aside in a separate account at the bank," Nicholas said. "Most likely, the late Lord Stafford made his wishes known at the bank, and they set up an account accordingly."

"So how is Stafford benefiting from Madalene's marriage?" Everett asked the group.

Mr. Swinton rose. "It's unclear, but we won't know until we find a copy of the will."

"Lady Madalene suggested that it was in Stafford's study," Everett said.

Holding up his hands in front of him, Mr. Swinton stated, "Bow Street Runners are not allowed to break into an estate. We uphold the law, not break it."

"Understood," Everett replied, glancing at Nicholas.

The Bow Street Runner bowed. "If you will excuse me, I will continue to search for leads on my end."

After Mr. Swinton stepped out of the room, Everett turned to Nicholas. "We need to break into Stafford's study."

"I agree, but it is much more difficult than you think to break into an estate."

Before he could respond, Hawkins stepped back into the room and announced, "Lady Madalene is eating breakfast in the dining room."

"Thank you, Hawkins," Everett acknowledged, striding towards the door.

Nicholas spoke up. "Where are you going?"

"To see Maddie."

He waved his hand. "Fine, go."

Walking across the entry hall, he arrived at the dining room and stopped outside the door. He took a moment to smooth out his cravat before he stepped inside and saw Madalene eating alone at the large table.

"Morning, Maddie."

She glanced over at him, and he saw the dark circles under her eyes, marring her beautiful features.

He rushed to her side. "Whatever is the matter?"

"I slept awful last night," she admitted, lowering her gaze to her lap.

Everett wanted to pull her into his arms like he had the night before, but he didn't dare. Instead, he crouched down next to her. "I hope you aren't too tired, because I have a fun day planned for us."

"You do?"

He leaned closer. "How would you like to go to the Royal Menagerie at the Tower today?"

She nibbled her bottom lip. "Do you believe it's safe?"

He nodded. "I do, truly."

"Then, I would love to," she said, her eyes brightening.

"Good," he replied. "I heard they have the most interesting bird collection."

She smiled broadly. "How exciting."

"Perhaps you can rest after breakfast, and I will come and collect you this afternoon," he suggested.

"Thank you," she murmured appreciatively.

"You are welcome." He returned her smile, knowing no further words were necessary. He would do anything to see her smile like that at him again.

Her piercing gaze watched him as he maintained eye contact, and he swore that time stopped. He was quite positive that he could get lost in her green eyes forever.

Penelope's voice broke through his thoughts. "Good morning, Everett. Would you care to join us for breakfast, or do you intend to continue staring at Madalene?" Her voice was full of mirth.

"I shall leave you ladies to your breakfast," he said, rising. "But I will be back in the afternoon to collect Madalene for a tour of the Royal Menagerie at the Tower."

Penelope gracefully sat down next to Madalene. "Would you like me to come along to chaperone?"

He wanted to shout no, but he responded with, "That won't be necessary. We shall ride in my barouche, which requires two footmen to attend us."

"Very good," Penelope said.

He bowed in their direction. "Until later, Maddie."

"I look forward to it." She smiled up at him.

Reluctantly, Everett started backing up. He found that he would much rather stay in Madalene's presence than go back to his estate and work on his ledgers. But the work of a marquess is never done.

Gripping her reticule in her lap, Madalene sat back in Everett's plush barouche. She had decided to wear a pale pink gown and kid boots for their excursion today. She snuck a peek at Everett, taking a moment to admire his clean-shaved jaw and trimmed sideburns.

Without a doubt, Everett was the most handsome man she had ever met. Not only was he attractive, but she felt a familiarity with him that she couldn't explain.

"Have you ever been to the Royal Menagerie?" he asked politely.

"I have not, but I have heard it's quite entertaining."

He nodded. "It is. The history of the Royal Menagerie is

fascinating as well. It's believed that lions were first kept in the tower during the reign of King John in about 1210. After that, his son, Henry III, established the menagerie, which included a polar bear and an elephant."

"Do you suppose the menagerie has an elephant on display today?"

"No," he responded. "Sadly, they haven't displayed an elephant for many years."

The barouche came to a stop, and a footman jumped down from the driver's bench. He came around and opened the door.

Everett hopped out and turned to assist her. As she placed her hand into his, she had a strong desire to never let it go. However, once she was securely on the pavement, Everett withdrew his hand.

"The beasts are kept in the western entrance of the tower," Everett shared, offering his arm to her.

Approaching the western entrance, they saw the figure of a lion over the door. Everett stopped in front of the door and rang a bell.

"This is where we pay our entrance fee, and the keeper will take us on a tour of the menagerie," he explained.

The door opened, and a red-headed man peeked out. "May I help you, sir?"

"We were hoping to take a tour of the grounds," Everett said.

"Of course." The man waved them inside. "My name is Mr. Mullens, and I am one of the keepers here."

Everett extended Mr. Mullens a few coins, and he deposited them into the pocket of his waistcoat. The keeper started walking across the cobblestone yard and spoke over his shoulder.

"We'll start with the wild beasts, particularly a lion and lioness from the Gulf of Persia."

Mr. Mullens led them down a flight of stairs to a spacious den. Iron grates enclosed the front of the dens, and the two lions were pacing back and forth.

"We are very proud of the cleanliness of the dens," the keeper said.

"As well you should be," Madalene replied. "These dens are very clean."

Mr. Mullens nodded in approval before he turned his attention back towards the lions. "These two are called Young Hector and Miss Jenny. They are three years old and are from the same litter. The Marquis Cornwallis presented them to his Majesty on the 6th of March 1800."

"They are exquisite animals," Everett admired.

Mr. Mullens agreed, "That they are." He pointed towards the next den where they saw a lion laying on its side. "This fine young lion was a gift from the Emperor of Morocco to the Duke of Kent and is extremely tame and docile." He smiled at the lion with pride. "This lion craves attention from the keepers."

"What is it like to be in the cage with these wild beasts?" Madalene questioned.

"It's necessary to remember that wild animals are unpredictable," Mr. Mullens shared. "You must never let your guard down."

Everett chuckled and muttered, "It sounds similar to dealing with the *ton*."

"Come, there are many more beasts to see," Mr. Mullens encouraged, walking towards the next den where a leopardess was pacing the cage. "This is Duchess. She was brought from the Malabar coast, and was gifted to his Majesty by Lord Carlisle."

Leaning closer, Madalene commented, "Her bright colors are magnificent."

Mr. Mullen placed his hand on her shoulder. "I urge you to be cautious not to step too close to the dens. Furthermore, I must insist you avoid every attempt to play with them."

Madalene turned and gave him a baffled look. "Who would attempt to play with these wild beasts?"

"You would be surprised," he remarked before he started walking down the path to another den.

Mr. Mullen spent the next hour or so regaling them with story after story about the different wild beasts and their unique histories. Amongst the wild beasts on display were tigers, a spotted hyena, a racoon, and even a bear from Greenland.

Stopping at the base of the stairs, Mr. Mullen put his hands out and announced, "That is the end of the official tour." He pointed up the stairs. "We do have a bird exhibit upstairs. Would you like to tour it?"

"I would, very much," Madalene said.

Mr. Mullen smiled. "You will be pleased to see a secretary bird in the exhibit."

"You have a secretary bird on display?" she said, her voice growing animated.

"We do," the keeper said. "It's in the Bird Room, which is where we used to house our monkeys. Just go up the stairs, and you can't miss it."

Pulling on Everett's arm, Madalene started leading him up the stairs towards the bird exhibit. They entered a large, crowded, brick room, which had cages along each wall housing birds of all sizes and colors.

She pointed towards a very large bird that had the appearance of an eagle, but had long, thin legs.

"That is a secretary bird," she said in an eager voice. "It is found only in Africa, and I have only seen pictures of them before."

Everett grinned. "It is a very large bird."

"It is," she murmured.

"Would you like me to purchase it for you?"

She gave him an exasperated look. "Don't be absurd, Everett. What would I do with a secretary bird?"

He shrugged. "If it will make you happy…" His voice trailed off, and she realized that he was being serious.

"That is a most gracious offer," she said, turning to face him. "But I want everyone to enjoy the secretary bird, not just myself."

"Do you find that this exhibit causes you to miss your father more?"

Her eyes scanned the birds for a moment before she spoke. "I miss my father every single day, and my mother as well. I miss the days when we ate supper as a family and took walks around our estate." She grew nostalgic at the memories.

Everett placed his hand over hers. "It sounds like you had a happy childhood."

"I did," she replied firmly.

"I am glad that you were close with your father."

She noticed that Everett's last words were laced with sadness. "Did you not have a good relationship with your father?"

"I did not," he admitted, his lips pressing tightly together. "My father was a very important man. He was constantly busy and did not have time for the rearing of children."

"That's not uncommon amongst aristocratic families."

He winced. "My father only had time for his *other* family."

"Oh," she breathed. "I am so sorry."

Shifting his gaze over her shoulder, he admitted, "My parents' marriage was one of convenience. Even though it was mostly harmonious, my father spent the majority of his time at his mistress's house across Town. One time, when I was home on holiday from Oxford, I followed my father to his mistress's townhouse and peered in the front window. I saw him embracing the younger children and handing them gifts."

"What an awful thing for you to witness," she expressed, knowing her words were inadequate.

"My father never embraced me, not once that I can remember," he admitted in a shaky voice. "He used to say that emotions were weaknesses."

"I disagree. I believe that displaying emotions is not a sign of weakness, but rather, a sign of strength."

Bringing his gaze back towards her, he shared, "After my father died, I saw his mistress and her three children visiting his grave. She appeared so grief-stricken that I approached her and spoke to her."

"What did she say?"

He frowned. "Apparently, my father hadn't made any provisions for her after his death, and she was evicted from her townhouse."

"That's awful."

"I agree. I felt like it was my duty to take care of this woman and her children," he said. "So, I purchased a small townhouse for her and offered her a generous settlement. If she is frugal, she will never have to work again."

Madalene's eyes met his, and she hoped he saw understanding and acceptance, not judgement. "That was admirable of you."

Everett stared at her for a long moment, then said, "You are an incredible woman, Maddie."

"Why do you say that?"

"Most women of the *ton* would be scandalized by even discussing my father's mistress, much less knowing that I supported her."

Madalene tightened her hold on his arm. "That's just ridiculous. Are we to pretend she doesn't exist?"

"My mother does," he said in a bitter tone.

"You must not judge your mother too harshly," Madalene stated. "She was in a difficult situation and coped the best way she knew how."

Everett furrowed his brow. "I hadn't thought about that before."

"To judge another is easy, but you never truly understand that person until you consider things from their point of view," she pressed.

He watched her, not saying anything, and she feared she'd gone too far. She opened her mouth to apologize, but he spoke first.

"You're right."

She grinned. "You sound surprised."

"No, I'm not," he said with a shake of his head. "I'm just curious how a beautiful woman became so wise at such a young age."

The way he spoke, she knew he was in earnest, and she ducked her head to hide her growing blush. "You mustn't say such flowery words to me."

"I must not speak the truth?"

She opened her mouth to speak when she saw a familiar face in the crowd. Lord Tattershell. He just stood there with a smirk on his face, watching her.

"It's him," she said in a hushed tone.

"Who?"

She pointed at him. "Lord Tattershell."

Everett turned and looked where she was pointing, but it was too late. Lord Tattershell had already disappeared back into the crowd.

"Are you sure it was him?"

Placing a hand on her hip, she stated, "I know what I saw."

"All right," he said in an appeasing tone.

She squared her shoulders. "Do not attempt to pacify me. I saw Lord Tattershell in the crowd."

"I believe you," he replied, placing a hand on her shoulder.

"Thank you," she mumbled as her eyes darted around the room.

Everett stepped back and offered his arm. "Perhaps it's time to end our little tour?" he suggested.

"I agree."

As Everett led her back to his barouche, Madalene found herself growing increasingly frustrated. He didn't seem to believe that Lord Tattershell was following her. Why didn't he?

For a day that had started off so promising, it had ended rather poorly.

10

Everett jogged down the stairs after another night of fitful sleep. Every time he closed his eyes, he remembered the hurt expression on Madalene's face after he questioned whether she'd truly seen Lord Tattershell. It had just seemed so inconceivable that he hadn't noticed Tattershell at the Royal Menagerie. The trip back to Hereford Hall had been filled with silence, and Madalene barely murmured a goodbye as she exited the barouche.

He needed to find a way to make it up to her. But how? He was fairly certain that women liked flowers. He would buy up every flower in London if he had to. He just wanted to see Madalene smile at him again.

"Everett, dear," his mother said from the entryway of the drawing room. "May I speak with you for a moment?"

He wanted to refuse her request, but seeing the expression on her face, he decided against it. "As you wish, Mother."

"Thank you," she said, stepping back into the drawing room.

As he entered, he saw his mother sitting down on the settee. "Come join me."

He complied, sitting next to her.

"Would you like a cup of tea?" she asked, pointing at the tea tray.

"No, thank you."

Lady Northampton sat back in her seat. "I missed you at breakfast this morning."

"I find I'm not hungry today."

Eyeing him with concern, she replied, "I can't help but notice that you seem out of sorts."

"I'm fine, Mother."

"Is this about Madalene?"

"Leave it alone," he replied sharply.

"Good heavens, Everett," she huffed. "I'm your mother, not a simpleton."

"I never implied you…"

With an imperious wave of her hand, she cut him off. "I know that your engagement to Madalene is a ruse."

He stared at her, dumbfounded. "How did you know?"

"I had my suspicions when you first told me, but I hoped I was wrong," she explained. "It was rather convenient for you to announce an engagement so soon after meeting Madalene, especially since you have had an aversion to marriage."

Shifting in his seat, Everett declared, "I don't have an aversion to marriage. I just don't care for it."

"Exactly," she replied. "Which is why I confirmed my suspicions with Madalene, and that poor girl couldn't lie to save her life. Although, she was rather convincing in the carriage."

"She was, wasn't she?"

"Which leads me to the conclusion that you are clearly smitten with each other," his mother stated, amusement in her tone.

Everett jumped up from his seat. "I am not smitten with Maddie. I care for the girl, but not in terms of marriage."

"I see," his mother said, pressing her lips together.

"You do not see, Mother," he proclaimed. "I want to give

Maddie the Season she deserves and allow her to pick her own suitor."

Mary sighed, clearly exasperated. "How does your plan work exactly? As far as the *ton* is concerned, you and Madalene have an understanding between you. No man would approach Lady Madalene for fear of offending *you*, the Marquess of Northampton."

"They will once she breaks the engagement off," he contended.

"And you would be all right with that?"

He nodded. "I will be."

Lady Northampton smiled. "Excellent. That's all I wanted to know."

"Pardon?"

She rose and walked over to a writing desk in the corner. "I have decided that I would like Hudson to marry Lady Madalene."

Everett blinked slowly. "You want my brother to marry Maddie?"

"I do," she admitted. "I'm quite fond of Madalene, and I believe that Hudson and she will suit nicely."

He took a commanding step towards her. "Absolutely not."

"Is there a reason they wouldn't, my dear?" she asked innocently, picking up a folded piece of paper from the desk.

Everett pursed his lips. He didn't have a good answer to that. He didn't know why they wouldn't suit; he just knew that they wouldn't.

"I've invited Hudson for a dinner party tomorrow evening," his mother informed him, appearing oblivious to his internal struggle. "I have also sent invitations to Lady Madalene, and the Duke and Duchess of Blackbourne."

Adjusting his grey riding jacket, Everett said, "I highly doubt Hudson will be able to escape his duties as a barrister for the evening."

"He's already accepted." Mary smiled victoriously at him.

"Delightful," he mumbled.

Lady Northampton eyed him with curiosity. "Isn't this what you intended all along? For Madalene to have her pick of suitors?"

"Yes, but…" Everett frowned. "I just hadn't considered that my brother would be one of those suitors."

"Wouldn't it be brilliant if they fell in love?" his mother gushed.

No, it wouldn't, he wanted to shout. Instead, he just forced a smile to his face. "If that will be all, I need to go speak to Maddie."

She waved her hand in front of her. "By all means, go. If Madalene isn't taken with Hudson, I suppose we could try your cousin, Gerald."

"Unacceptable!" he shouted. "Gerald is a known rake. Madalene is not to go anywhere near him!" Everett's tone brooked no argument.

"You make a valid point." His mother pulled out the chair at the writing desk and sat down. "There are many gentlemen of the *ton* that I can recommend for Madalene. I could even host a ball in her honor."

Everett's jaw was clenched so tightly that he could barely speak. "No ball," he found himself growling.

"Didn't you say that you wanted Madalene to have a Season?" she asked, glancing over at him.

"I did but…"

She cut him off. "A ball in her honor would allow her to be properly presented to Society."

"That's not necessary."

Picking up a quill, his mother objected, "You're keeping her tucked away, Everett. Madalene needs an opportunity to meet potential suitors."

"You will not defy me on this, Mother. I said, 'no ball'," he proclaimed before storming out the door.

What was his infuriating mother thinking, he wondered as he grabbed the top hat from his butler's hands. Hudson and Maddie would never suit. *Ever*. Hudson may be charming, but he was buried in his work as a barrister. Maddie needed someone that would spend time with her, making her feel cherished. Hudson was most assuredly *not* that man.

And he was *not* keeping Maddie tucked away from Society. He had taken her to the theatre and the Royal Menagerie. She didn't need to have a ball. The terrifying image of Maddie dancing with other men came into his mind. Why did it bother him so much? After all, they were just friends, nothing more.

Madalene was sitting at the writing desk as she attempted to compose a note to Isabella. Crumbled pieces of paper surrounded her, because she couldn't seem to come up with the right wording. How did one tell their dear friend that they were engaged to their brother, but that it was all just one big ruse? Perhaps it might be best for her to wait till the end of the Season to explain everything.

Besides, she was still angry at Everett, and Isabella might pick up on that in her letter. How dare he not believe her? They were friends, and they should trust each other. After all, she trusted him. But he didn't trust her. What a horrible feeling of betrayal.

"I know that look," Penelope said as she walked into the room. "You're still angry at Everett."

"I am," Madalene replied, seeing no reason to deny it.

The duchess sat on a settee near her. "You must understand that men think differently than women. We must be patient with them."

"Think differently? In what way?"

"For example, Nicholas has a solemn personality, but he truly is kind and gentle. He may say things in a way that seems hurtful, but he has good intentions behind his words."

Madalene placed the quill next to the inkpot. "The duke has been most kind and gracious to allow me to stay at Hereford Hall."

"He has no choice," Penelope responded with a smirk. "Nicholas would do anything to make me happy." She paused. "Much like Everett would do for you."

Fingering the neckline of her light blue gown, Madalene replied, "But it's an entirely different situation than yours and the duke's. After all, Everett and I are just friends."

"Are you sure about that?"

Madalene nodded. "We are."

Penelope gave her a look that seemed to indicate she didn't believe her.

"We are just friends," Madalene repeated for emphasis.

The duchess rose from her seat. "All right then, your *friend* is in the entry hall with a bouquet of flowers for you."

"He brought me flowers?" Madalene asked, surprised.

Penelope smiled. "Because, apparently, that is what friends do, bring flowers to each other."

Madalene rose from her seat. "Everett just views me as a woman that needs rescuing, not as anything more."

"Interesting," Penelope murmured. "I fear that you are mistaken."

"I am not mistaken. I'm speaking the truth."

Penelope looped her arm through Madelene's. "Come, let's go down and meet your *friend*."

As they walked down the hall, Madalene kept replaying Penelope's words in her mind. Could Everett have started developing feelings for her? No. That was impossible.

They turned the corner, and she saw Everett standing in the

entry hall with a bouquet of flowers in his hand. When he saw her, his eyes lit up and a smile came to his face.

"Lady Madalene," he said as he approached, then stopped and held the bouquet of flowers out to her. "These are for you."

"Thank you." She accepted the flowers and brought them to her nose. "They smell lovely."

Everett appeared stiff as he watched her, and if she had to guess, vulnerable.

"Would you care to take a turn around the gardens?" he asked hopefully.

She smiled graciously. "Of course."

"I'll take the flowers and ensure they're placed in a vase," Penelope said, reaching for them. "Just as a reminder, Nicholas and I will be chaperoning from his study window."

Everett offered his arm, and they slowly made their way towards the gardens behind the townhouse. Meandering stone paths, bright pockets of flowers, and prim holly hedges dominated the garden landscape.

Everett frowned as she dropped his arm and created more distance between them.

"How did you sleep?" he asked.

"Well," she lied. "And you?"

"Horribly."

She glanced over at him. "I'm sorry."

"Do you want to know why?"

"Why?"

He stopped and turned to face her. "Because of you."

"Me?"

He jabbed his fingers through his hair. "I offended you when I questioned whether you'd truly seen Tattershell." He stepped closer to her. "I'm sorry, Maddie."

Looking deep into his blue eyes, she realized that she could never stay mad at him. "You're forgiven."

"Truly?"

"Truly," she replied.

He sighed deeply. "Thank you. You've made me immensely happy."

Reaching into the pocket of her gown, she removed a folded piece of paper. "Were you aware that your Mother is throwing a dinner party tomorrow evening?"

"So I've just discovered."

She slipped the paper back into her pocket. "And did Lady Northampton reveal that she discovered that our engagement was a ruse?"

"She did," he confirmed.

Madalene turned, admiring the trees lining the length of the gardens. "She's much more clever than you gave her credit for."

"That she is," he admitted. "She even invited my brother, Hudson, for the festivities."

A smile came to Madalene's face at that unexpected news. "Is this the brother in the Royal Navy or the barrister?"

"The barrister."

"What an exciting profession."

"Is it?" Everett replied in a doubtful tone. "It appears rather dull to me."

"Not everything can be as exciting as being a marquess," she teased.

"Good point."

Her eyes lingered on the beech trees with their large, low-hanging branches. "Would you care to climb a tree?" she asked, holding her breath for his response.

"Now?"

Madalene nodded eagerly.

"But you're in a dress."

She shrugged nonchalantly. "I always climb in dresses."

For a moment he didn't speak, but then he gestured towards the trees. "Which one would you recommend?"

"You must pick a tree with large, strong branches that will be able to support your weight," she explained as they walked over to a beech tree. Stopping in front of it, she continued, "You should always inspect the lower trunk, looking for any signs of a damaged or dying tree."

"I'm afraid I missed that step as a youth," Everett remarked jovially as he removed his jacket and laid it on the ground. He made a point of inspecting the tree. "This appears to be a good one."

"It is." Reaching up, she grabbed a low-hanging branch and pulled herself up. "Make sure you tug on each branch before putting your weight on it." She moved up to the next branch. "And be cautious where you place your feet."

As she climbed the tree, she heard Everett below her, but she kept going until she reached a good resting spot. Pulling herself up, she leaned her back against the thick tree trunk.

"You are remarkably agile for a woman wearing a dress," Everett teased as he pulled himself up onto the branch next to her.

"It comes with a lot of practice." Madalene breathed a contented sigh as she closed her eyes. She listened to the birds chirping in the tree next to them. "This is my haven," she murmured after a moment.

"I worry that you might fall and break your neck one of these days," he said in a serious voice.

"That won't happen," she assured him.

A peaceful silence descended over them as they listened to the wind blowing through the trees. The silence was short-lived, however.

"My mother intends to throw you a ball," Everett announced unexpectedly.

"A ball?"

"Yes. How would you feel about that?" he asked, turning to look at her.

A smile formed on her lips. "I would love one."

"You would?"

She lifted her brow. "Why wouldn't I?"

"Her intention is to introduce you to Society so you can meet eligible bachelors."

"Oh?" she responded, confused at his reluctance. Wasn't that their intention all along? "Do you think I should?"

"Meet eligible bachelors?"

Madalene laughed. "More specifically, have your mother host a ball for me with that intention. Do you think it's a good idea?"

"Whatever will make you happy, Maddie," he replied tenderly.

Glancing over at him, she mused, "It does sound rather enjoyable."

"Then, so be it," he replied. "I'll let my mother know you approve."

"Thank you, Everett."

He grew quiet, then spoke softly. "We both know this engagement is a ruse. At the end of the Season, we shall go our separate ways."

"What if I don't want to go separate ways?" she asked.

"Then, I shall be honor bound to marry you, Maddie." His words sounded forced.

She huffed in response. "What I meant was that I hope we can remain friends, even after the end of the Season."

"Ah," he replied. "We shall always be friends."

Leaning the back of her head against the trunk of the tree, Madalene closed her eyes. Penelope had been wrong, much to her dismay. It was now evident that Everett only viewed her as a friend. She heard the way he choked out the words about being forced to marry her. He most definitely did not hold any affection for her.

11

Sitting alone in his study, Everett reviewed the ledgers his man of business had given him. He wasn't making much progress, though. He kept reading the same line over and over. His thoughts were continuously plagued by Madalene. Why had he encouraged her to have a ball? He shouldn't have said anything. But that wouldn't have been fair to Maddie. He'd done the right thing, so why did he feel anger stirring up inside of him?

"Howe informed me that you wanted to see me," his mother said as she entered.

"I do," he replied, rising from his chair. "Please sit down."

She looked perplexed as she sat in front of him. "I missed you at supper last night."

"My apologies. I should have sent word that Penelope invited me to stay for supper. Afterwards, we played cards till late in the evening."

"And for breakfast?"

"I decided to go riding this morning." He sat down. "I spoke to Maddie, and she shared that she'd like you to host a ball for her."

"But I thought you said…"

Everett spoke over her. "I know what I said, but I changed my mind." He sat back in his chair.

"How do you feel about that, Son?"

He gave her a blank stare. "Why does it matter how I feel about it? It would be a ball for Maddie, not me."

"And you don't have any reservations about Madalene mingling with other gentlemen of the *ton*?"

"None." He nearly choked on the word.

For a moment, he thought his mother was going to press the subject, but then a bright smile came to her face. "Excellent. I shall start planning immediately!" she exclaimed eagerly. "It shall be the event of the Season."

"I'd prefer a more intimate affair."

Ignoring him, Lady Northampton continued, "We shall have a full orchestra and chalked designs on the dance floor."

"Mother…" he warned.

She started walking towards the door, ticking off the list of preparations on her fingers. "How exciting! We'll need to open up the ball room, and I'll need to start sending out invitations…"

The butler interrupted from the doorway. "His grace, the Duke of Blackbourne, is here to see you, milord."

"Send him in."

Immediately, Nicholas stepped through the doorway with his top hat in his left hand.

"Nicholas, what a pleasant surprise," Lady Northampton greeted.

The duke stepped over to her and kissed her on the cheek. "You're looking well, Mary. Quite cheerful, in fact."

"Thank you," she replied gleefully. "Madalene has agreed that I should host a ball in her honor."

"Truly?" Nicholas asked, arching an eyebrow.

Mary smiled. "Isn't it grand? I intend to invite all the eligible bachelors in Town, and Madalene shall have her pick of suitors."

"What a brilliant idea!" Nicholas declared. "That way, Everett won't be shackled to Madalene at the end of the Season."

Mary nodded approvingly. "Indeed. If you will excuse me, I shall start creating a guest list." She beamed at her son before she departed.

Nicholas turned an incredulous gaze towards Everett. "Have you gone mad?"

"Pardon?"

Stepping closer to the desk, Nicholas asked, "You would willingly allow Madalene to mingle with other gentlemen of the ton?"

"Why wouldn't I?"

Nicholas huffed as he placed his top hat on a nearby chair. "You are an imbecile. There's no greater misery than watching the woman you care about dancing with another."

"As you well know, this engagement is a ruse…"

"That's rubbish," Nicholas objected, cutting him off.

Everett closed the ledger in front of him. "Be that as it may be, Maddie was pleased by the prospect of a ball." He lifted his brow. "Can we drop the subject now?"

Nicholas watched him for a long moment, then shared, "Mr. Swinton visited me early this morning with some rather interesting news."

"Did he find a copy of the will?"

"No," Nicholas replied, shaking his head. "But he did inform me that Tattershell has a list of creditors who are demanding that he be thrown into debtor's prison."

"Truly?"

"Furthermore, the Bow Street runner that has been assigned to Tattershell, confirmed that he has been following Lady Madalene."

"For what purpose?"

Nicholas grew solemn. "There's a good chance that Tattershell intends to abduct her and flee to Gretna Greens."

"Not if I can help it," Everett growled.

"My sentiments exactly," Nicholas replied. "Between us, we will keep her safe."

Pursing his lips, Everett admitted, "I was a fool not to believe Maddie when she told me that she saw Tattershell at the Royal Menagerie."

"By not marrying Madalene, he has lost £30,000," Nicholas remarked. "He'll be hard pressed to find another heiress of her worth this Season."

"Has Swinton located Lord Stafford's solicitor?"

Nicholas nodded. "He has. A Mr. Ezra Cooke."

"Does he, by chance, have a copy of the late Earl Stafford's will?"

"No," Nicholas replied with a shake of his head. "He claims that no will exists."

The two men sat in silence for a moment.

"Would you care to go riding?" Nicolas asked.

"Thank you, but no." Everett shook his head. "I went earlier, and now I have a stack of work that needs to be tended to."

Nicholas rose, picked up his top hat, and placed it on his head. "Well, I shall be off then. I'll see you at the dinner party this evening."

"Don't remind me," Everett grumbled. "Hudson is coming."

"Splendid! I haven't seen Hudson in years."

"He hasn't changed much."

"Other than now being a highly sought-after barrister," Nicholas pointed out. "I often read about his cases in the morning newspapers."

Finished with this conversation, Everett picked up his quill from the inkpot. "If you'll excuse me, I have work to do."

Nicholas chuckled. "I'll see you tonight."

Everett watched as his friend left the room. He didn't know why he suddenly felt jealous of his brother. After all, he was the Marquess of Northampton, and his brother was just a barrister.

Then again, perhaps he did know why. Ladies had always fawned over Hudson, and he didn't want Maddie to fall for his younger brother, too.

Dressed in an elegant pink gown with a modest neckline and puffy sleeves, Madalene sat at the dressing room table as her lady's maid styled her hair.

"Did you enjoy yourself at the Royal Menagerie?" Amy asked enthusiastically.

"I did."

"What was your favorite beast?"

Madalene took a moment to consider her response. "I would have to say the black leopard."

Amy nodded in approval. "That sounds lovely. I can't wait to visit the Royal Menagerie, but first I need to save up a shilling for the entrance fee. My older sister, Leah, has gone on the tour, and she told me how exciting it was. My father told me that there used to be a monkey room where you were able to feed and hold the monkeys." She paused for only a moment before continuing. "Can you imagine holding a monkey in your hand?"

"I cannot," Madalene replied, surprised she was able to get a word in.

Her lady's maid walked over to the hearth and picked up the curling tongs. "If I had to pick my favorite beast, I'd have to say it would be a lion."

"Have you ever seen a lion?"

Amy shook her head as she reached for a lock of her hair to curl. "No, milady, but I have seen sketches of them."

"They are majestic creatures," Madalene admitted.

"I would imagine so," Amy said, stepping to her other side. "I have seen a hedgehog, though."

"A hedgehog?" Madalene repeated.

Amy released the curled lock of hair and reached for another. "They're found in the woodlands where I grew up. They are funny-looking creatures and have spikes on their backs. If you try to pick one up, their needles stab you." She went to place the curling tongs down on the hearth. "They aren't poisonous, but it hurts something fierce."

Madalene smiled. "I take it that you know from experience."

"Yes, milady." Amy giggled. "I did convince my brother to pick one up once. He let out a howl and wouldn't speak to me for days." Placing a hand on Madalene's shoulder, she giggled again. "Those were the best days of my life."

Amy picked up some tiny pink flowers from the dressing table and began entwining them into Madalene's hair. "My mother wasn't too pleased, but I figured my brother deserved it for all the pranks he'd played on me."

"It sounds as if your family is close," Madalene commented.

"That we are," her lady's maid replied. "After my father died, me and my siblings found jobs. My mother is sick and can't work anymore. I've worked my way up from a kitchen maid to a house maid. Now, look at me. I'm a lady's maid."

Amy took a step back and smiled approvingly. "You look lovely, Lady Madalene."

Rising, Madalene returned Amy's infectious smile and decided she wanted to do something nice for her.

"I want to give you something, Amy." She picked up her reticule, pulled out a shilling, and extended it towards her. "I want you to go to the menagerie and report back to me what your favorite beast was."

Amy eyed the coin with interest, but then she shook her head. "I don't take charity, milady."

"Good," she replied, "this isn't charity. I want you to go and tell me if a lion is more magnificent than a black leopard."

Glancing down at the offered shilling, Amy frowned. "It still feels like charity."

"It's an order," Madalene replied in a mock stern tone.

Amy nodded, then reached out and accepted the coin, clasping it tightly in her hand. "Thank you, Lady Madalene. I shall go at once."

Madalene turned her head to admire her hair style in the mirror. "You've done a splendid job on my hair."

"Thank you," Amy murmured as she picked up the kid gloves off the dressing table and extended them towards her.

As Madalene started pulling on the gloves, a knock came at the door. Before she could answer, it opened, revealing Penelope.

The duchess stepped into the room wearing a green gown with a square neckline. "Are you ready to depart?"

"I am," Madalene replied.

"You look positively radiant, Maddie."

"Thank you." Madalene smiled as they moved toward the staircase.

Nicholas was waiting for them in the entry hall. "You're looking well tonight, Madalene."

She curtsied. "Thank you, your grace."

"I believe I asked you to call me Nicholas," he reminded her.

"You have," she replied, offering him a smile, "multiple times, in fact."

"Come, it's time for us to go," Penelope said, accepting Nicholas's offered arm.

Madalene trailed after them and sat across from Penelope and Nicholas in the coach. She gazed out the window, but the night air did little to ease the stuffiness of the coach. Removing the fan from her reticule, she started fanning her face.

Everett's townhouse was only a few blocks away, and she was immensely grateful that it was such a short distance. The coach came to a stop, and Nicholas assisted the ladies out. The moment she stepped onto the pavement, the door to the townhouse opened, and Everett rushed down the steps to greet her.

"You've finally arrived," he greeted, stopping in front of her, which gave her a moment to admire his black jacket and matching trousers, his bright white waistcoat, and white cravat.

She arched an eyebrow. "That greeting makes me believe you must have missed me."

"I have," he replied, offering his arm. "Did you miss me?"

Sliding her gloved hand into the crook of his elbow, she cheekily remarked, "Does a horse miss a burr under the saddle?"

"You wound me, my fair maiden," he said, dramatically placing his free hand over his heart.

"I have no doubt your ego will recover soon enough, my lord."

He chuckled as he led her up the steps and into the townhouse, trailing behind Penelope and Nicholas.

Madalene stopped in the entry hall and admired the ornate woodwork running the length of the ivory-colored walls, the richly painted ceiling, and the numerous works of art hanging throughout the hall. A grandiose staircase dominated the far side of the room.

"Your townhouse is exquisite," she breathed.

Puffing out his chest in pride, Everett said, "The numerous works of art, wall paintings, and sculptures have been in my family for generations, if not centuries."

"On my last visit to my ancestral estate, I noticed that my uncle had sold off some of the family tapestries and paintings," she admitted reluctantly.

Everett glanced at her. "It must have been awful for you to lose those family heirlooms."

"It was. What was worse was that he moved my mother's portrait up into the attic."

"I'm sorry," he murmured.

"Oh well," Madalene said, attempting to keep the wistfulness out of her tone. "I should just be grateful that he didn't sell it."

Everett turned to face her, keeping her hand securely tucked into the crook of his arm. "You don't have to be brave around me, Maddie."

She hesitated, then replied, "But I do."

"Why?" he asked, his eyes imploring.

"If you saw the true me, you would know how weak and tired I am of being alone."

"You are not alone."

She lowered her gaze. "I am. My parents are gone, and I am forced to rely on the charity of others to survive."

He placed his left hand under her chin, forcing her to look at him. "It's a privilege to help a friend in need."

"Why are you being so kind to me?" she asked earnestly, her eyes roaming his devastatingly handsome face.

He flashed her a flirtatious smile. "Because we're engaged, remember?"

"Do be serious."

Everett's smile dimmed, but it was not lost entirely. He placed his free hand on top of hers. "I suppose I felt responsible for you the moment you fell into my curricle."

She smiled. "I must admit, I'm glad I chose your curricle."

"As am I." He dropped his hand from her chin and stepped to the side. "We'd better hurry or the others will start to search for us."

Everett led her across the entry hall and down a narrow hall. Stepping into the drawing room, Madalene barely had a moment to admire the large murals on the walls when she was approached by Lady Northampton and a handsome young man whose features were very similar to Everett's.

She felt Everett tense as his mother and brother approached. That's an odd reaction, she thought.

"Lady Madalene, welcome," Lady Northampton said, stopping in front of her. "Allow me the honor of introducing my son, Lord Hudson Beauchamp."

Madalene started to remove her hand from the crook of Everett's arm, but he still had a hand on top of hers and didn't release his hold. Feeling confused, she looked up at him. His expression was unreadable. He seemed to be staring at something on the other side of the room, so she tugged her hand free, then faced Lord Hudson and curtsied.

"It's a pleasure to meet you, Lord Hudson."

Bowing, he reached for her gloved hand and brought it up to his lips. "Truly, the moon hides her face when confronted with your beauty, Lady Madalene," he said in a deep, baritone voice.

Madalene swore she heard a growl come from the back of Everett's throat, but when she glanced up at him again, she saw that his attention was still directed elsewhere.

"You're too kind," she replied, smiling at his brother.

"There's nothing kind about it," Lord Hudson assured her as he released her hand.

Lady Northampton smiled approvingly as she glanced between them. "I was just speaking to Hudson about your many accomplishments."

"Is that so?" Madalene replied politely.

Hudson nodded. "She was, endlessly," he said. "I've heard that you are fluent in multiple languages, excel at needlework, and are proficient at watercolors."

"I would hardly call myself proficient at watercolors," Madalene replied with a smile.

"And if my memory serves me correctly, you are Isabella's friend, the talented tree climber."

"I am," Madalene stated, seeing no reason to deny it.

She expected to see judgment on his face, but instead he leaned closer. "I think that's brilliant."

"You do?"

"I do, especially since I intend to challenge you to a tree race one of these days."

"What exactly would a tree race entail?" she asked, curious.

"It's simple, really. We both pick out a tree and the first one who climbs up to the top wins."

Madalene grinned. "I accept your challenge, but I feel inclined to inform you that you'll lose."

Hudson tsked. "I think not. I'm a master tree climber. I bested my brothers all the time."

"That's not true," Everett objected.

Nicholas spoke up from behind Hudson. "I must side with Hudson on this one. Since we were young, I've never seen another climb up a tree with such precision."

Lady Northampton clasped her hands together. "We shall have to finish this lively discussion over dinner. Shall we?"

Before Madalene could even blink, Hudson had his arm extended towards her. "May I escort you in to dinner, Lady Madalene?"

Her eyes darted to Everett, and she saw that he wasn't pleased by his brother's offer. But to decline would be rude.

"Thank you," she replied, tentatively placing her hand on top of his arm.

As they walked down the hall, Hudson remarked, "I understand that you just finished your coursework at Miss Bell's Finishing School."

"I did."

"Forgive me, but I must pose a question," he began dramatically. "Is my sister still riding astride?"

Madalene laughed. "Yes, much to the chagrin of Miss Bell." She lowered her voice to admit, "At one point, Miss Bell ordered all saddles to be tucked away, except for side saddles, of course."

"Of course."

"However, Isabella got around that rule by riding without a saddle at all."

Hudson tossed his head back and laughed. "That sounds exactly like Isabella."

They entered a rectangular room with a vaulted ceiling and red-papered walls. A large chandelier hung down over the center of the oval table.

From behind them, Lady Northampton shared, "I decided to make use of the family dining room rather than our formal one. I feel it's more intimate."

Hudson led her to a chair and pulled it out. Once she was situated, he claimed the seat next to her, and Lady Northampton came to sit on her other side. Everett sat next to his brother with Nicholas to his side.

"Allow me," Hudson said, picking up the napkin and draping it into her lap.

"Thank you," she replied, feeling herself flushing just a little.

He winked. "It's my honor, my lady."

Good heavens, she thought. Hudson was boldly flirting with her, and she found herself nervously glancing at Everett. However, he seemed deep in conversation with Nicholas. The thought came to her that Everett was just her friend, not truly her fiancé. She had every right to enjoy conversing with Hudson.

After all, this had been their plan all along.

12

"If I recall correctly," Madalene said, turning her attention towards Hudson, "I believe Everett told me that you are a barrister."

"I am."

"What an interesting choice of profession."

"It is." He reached for his glass. "I attended Oxford before I applied to the Inns of Court. I was fortunate enough to study under Lord Herbert Moore, and after a few years, I was called to the bar."

A footman placed a bowl of soup in front of her. She smiled her thanks, then looked back at Hudson. "Do you enjoy presenting cases in court?"

"I do, very much. Although, the stench can be overwhelming at times," Hudson explained. "The courtrooms are sprinkled with herbs and flowers to mask the smell of unwashed prisoners."

"Is it true that much of the courts' daily business is conducted in Latin?" Penelope asked.

"Yes, your grace." He took a sip of his drink. "That can be confusing to most of the citizens, however. Most of my cases involve street robbery, petty thievery, drunk and disorderly behavior, and poaching. Not exactly the most educated people."

"That sounds rather dull."

He grinned. "It is. However, I have tried a few murder cases."

"Murder?" Penelope repeated, her eyebrows raised. "That sounds rather exciting."

"Indeed," he replied. "One of my first murder cases revolved around an old lady claiming to have heard a ghost wailing in the night. She was adamant that a ghost was haunting their town. She even went so far as to report the ghost to the constable, but he did not pursue the issue. He claimed a ghost haunting a town was balderdash. So, this lady riled up the townsfolk and encouraged everyone to arm themselves."

Madalene found herself leaning closer in anticipation. "What happened next?"

"Unfortunately," he continued, "a young child was playing in some laundry and draped a white sheet over his body. When the woman came across what she thought was a ghost, she pulled out her pistol and shot the child dead."

"That poor child," Penelope murmured.

Hudson nodded in agreement. "It was an unfortunate accident, but the old lady was arrested and brought to trial, anyway. She attempted to use her influence as the daughter of a baron. However, she was found guilty of murder and was sentenced to hang."

"Was she hung?"

He shook his head. "I successfully argued that she was mad, so she was sent to Bedlam Hospital to serve out her life sentence."

"That was most kind of you to save the woman's life," Madalene expressed.

Shrugging, he responded, "It was my privilege." With a side

glance at Everett, he leaned closer to her and lowered his voice. "I would much rather talk about you, Lady Madalene."

"What would you like to know?"

"I am most curious about how you and my brother became acquainted."

She reached for her spoon, then shared, "I fell out of a tree into his curricle."

"You fell out of a tree… intentionally?"

"I did."

He lifted his brow. "May I ask what you were doing in a tree in the first place?"

"I was running away from my horrid fiancé and uncle."

"I see. Well, at least you had a valid reason for being there," he said. "So, my brother rescued you from their clutches and brought you to safety in London?"

"Very good, barrister." Madalene smirked.

Hudson chuckled. "You are a cheeky thing, Lady Madalene."

"Everett was kind enough to provide me a ride to Hereford Hall," she explained. "Then, the duchess hired me as her companion."

Penelope held up her glass and declared, "And Madalene has been an excellent companion so far."

"You are her companion?" Hudson asked, looking confused. "I thought you were engaged to my brother."

"She is," Everett grunted from his seat.

"Currently, I am both," Madalene replied, putting her spoon down. "You see, my uncle, Lord Stafford, demanded that I marry Lord Tattershell…"

"You were engaged to Tattershell? And Lord Stafford is your uncle?" Hudson groaned, cutting her off. "No wonder you ran away!"

"Exactly. However, my uncle was insistent that I marry Tattershell, and Everett offered for me instead."

Hudson bobbed his head in approval. "That does not surprise

me. My brother has always been a true gentleman, especially when it comes to the ladies."

Madalene smiled at Everett. "That he is."

"I have to ask. Did you use witchcraft on my brother?" Hudson asked sarcastically.

"Why?"

Hudson grinned. "I never thought I'd see the day when he'd offer for a woman. He's always had an aversion to marriage."

"That's not true," Everett grumbled.

Nicholas spoke up from his side of the table. "It is true. Women fall at your feet, but you barely give them any heed. It's almost as if you're immune to their charms."

"This is coming from a man that ordered his wife to marry him," Everett countered.

Nicholas grinned. "That should tell you something."

Glancing between them, Hudson commented, "However, Mother has informed me that you two are not truly engaged, that it's a ruse to help keep Madalene safe from her uncle."

"That's partially true," Everett admitted after a long pause. "I wanted to give Maddie a Season, and I have no doubt that she'll soon have many suitors vying for her attention."

"I agree," Hudson said, his eyes lingering on her face. "You are the daughter of an earl with an impressive dowry, and you have the face of an angel."

Madalene felt a blush creep into her cheeks.

Everett scowled into his now empty soup bowl.

Turning his attention towards the duke, Hudson said, "I understand the Americans have invaded Upper Canada at Sandwich."

"It's true," Nicholas replied. "But I have no doubt that our troops will quickly put down this skirmish once and for all."

"Our brother, Dudley is a lieutenant on the fourteen-gun HMS *Penance*, and, last we heard, is fighting off the American coast," Hudson shared.

"Ah, he is serving under Captain Monroe, then, " Nicholas said. "He's a fine man, and an even better captain."

Lady Northampton let out a relieved sigh. "That does provide me with some comfort. It's disheartening to know my son is fighting those troublesome Americans."

"I completely agree, especially since the real war is being fought in the Peninsula," Nicholas commented as a footman reached for his empty bowl.

Just then, two footmen walked in with trays of mutton and placed them in the center of the table.

"Allow me," Hudson said as he reached over and carved off a small piece of mutton, placing it on Madalene's plate.

"Thank you," she replied, enjoying the delicious aroma of the meat. "Everett mentioned that you crafted a few boats when you were younger."

Hudson laughed as he placed a large piece of mutton on his own plate. "We begged our parents to buy us a boat to use on the pond near our estate, but they refused. So, we took it into our own hands." He grinned. "We cut down some trees and made our first attempt that summer."

Everett chuckled. "That one sunk as soon as we placed it in the water."

"That it did," Hudson confirmed, "but we were wiser with each attempt. Eventually, we crafted a boat that carried all three of us along with our fishing equipment. We'd just made it to the middle of the pond, when the boat started taking on water."

"We had to jump overboard, taking our fishing equipment into the water with us," Everett shared. "Our parents were furious, because we came home soaking wet."

"It's true," Hudson responded.

Lady Northampton shook her head in amusement. "What my boys failed to mention was that we forbade them from swimming in that murky pond, but they gave us no heed. I doubt there were even fish in that body of water."

Turning towards Everett, Hudson remarked, “If I recall, you took the brunt of father’s anger that day.”

“I always did. Father held me to a higher standard as the heir,” Everett replied sternly.

Despite his tone, Madalene couldn’t help hearing the wistfulness of his words, and she glanced over at him in concern. He met her gaze and offered her a weak smile. It was evident that his father’s rejection hurt him more than he let on.

Hudson shifted towards her. “After dinner, would you care to take a turn around the drawing room with me?”

She couldn’t help but notice that Everett was watching her closely. “I suppose so,” she replied.

Hudson smiled at her. “Excellent. I shall look forward to it.”

Once the footmen cleared the main course, salad and cheese were placed in front of them.

Glancing over at Everett, she saw his jaw was clenched so tightly that a muscle pulsated under his ear. She didn’t understand him at all. At times, he flirted with her and seemed to hold her in affection, but the next moment, he would keep her at a distance. It was perplexing and very frustrating.

The moment his mother announced that the ladies would retire to the drawing room, Everett shoved back his chair and rose. He quickly stepped over to Madalene and assisted her in rising.

“Thank you,” she murmured softly.

Taking her hand, he tucked it into the crook of his arm. “Will you allow me the privilege of walking you to the drawing room?”

Madalene opened her mouth to speak when Lady Northampton spoke up. “That won’t be necessary, Everett. I shall walk Madalene to the drawing room. Why don't you escort the men to your study for a glass of port?"

Hudson placed a hand on his shoulder. "Come on, Brother. We shall join the ladies later for some whist."

"Ladies, I have some handkerchiefs laid out for us to embroider while the gentlemen are enjoying their port," Lady Northampton insisted gently.

Begrudgingly, Everett allowed Madalene to withdraw her hand from his arm. He didn't want to go drink port with the men. He would prefer to adjourn to the drawing room with Maddie and play a rousing game of whist.

Madalene smiled up at Everett. "I feel I should warn you that I am most proficient at whist."

"Are you now?" he asked, returning her smile.

"I am."

Nicholas interjected, "Whist is about strategy, and as a former captain in His Majesty's Royal Navy, I'm a serious strategist."

"I wouldn't count Madalene or myself out just yet," Penelope declared. "At Miss Bell's Finishing School, we spent many hours playing card games and tossing dice. Miss Bell felt it was an important part of our education to be well-versed in games played in the drawing room."

"Enough debate," Lady Northampton said. "Ladies, follow me." She turned on her heel and walked out of the room.

Penelope looped her hand through Madalene's and led her towards the door.

Once he lost sight of Maddie, Everett headed towards his study, knowing his brother and Nicholas would follow. He stepped into the room and walked over to the drink cart.

"This room holds so many memories for me," Hudson said as he entered. His eyes scanned the intricate woodwork running along the walls and the mural painted above the fireplace.

Everett took the lid off the decanter. “I haven’t changed it much since I inherited the townhouse.”

“I can tell. This room is exactly how I remember it,” Hudson remarked.

“You should come visit more often,” Everett encouraged, pouring port into three glasses.

“I’ve been awfully busy,” his brother stated. “I’m working towards becoming a high court judge.”

Nicholas stepped up and accepted a glass of port. “Aren’t you too young for that position?”

“I am,” Hudson replied, “but it takes years to become a high court judge. Recently, I was nominated to become a district judge, and I’ve accepted.”

Everett extended him a glass. “That’s wonderful news. Have you told Mother yet?”

“Not yet,” Hudson answered, then sipped his port.

“She’ll be overjoyed,” Everett stated.

“That she will be.” Hudson lowered his glass, looking thoughtful. “I’ve been working so diligently at my professional responsibilities that I haven’t had time to court any young ladies.” He paused. “I think it’s time I settle down and produce an heir.”

“You’re still young,” Everett replied, not pleased at the turn of this conversation.

“If you’re not opposed, I’d like your permission to court Lady Madalene,” Hudson said, looking at his brother.

“Absolutely not!” Everett exclaimed.

Hudson frowned. “Mother informed me that you two don’t really have an understanding, despite what’s being spread around the *ton*.”

“That’s true,” he replied. “But my answer is *no*.”

“May I ask why?”

Everett wanted to shout his objections. Instead, he attempted a more rational approach. “Think of Maddie’s reputation. It would be unseemly for her to break the engagement off with me, only to become engaged to my younger brother."

Twirling the drink in his hand, Hudson looked thoughtful. "I disagree. Madalene is a beautiful young woman. I have no doubt the *ton* will embrace her once they see that we are a love match."

"You and Maddie are not a love match," Everett scoffed. "It takes years for two people to fall in love."

Nicholas placed his empty glass down on the drink cart. "I believe it only takes a moment for two people to fall in love, but you spend the rest of your days cultivating that love."

Everett shook his head as he took a sip of his port. "Maddie is mine…"

"Yours?" Hudson asked, speaking over him. "I thought you said in the dining room…"

Everett cut his brother off. "I know what I said, but you can't have her."

Reaching for the decanter, Hudson asked, "Do you intend to marry her at the end of the Season, then?"

"Perhaps."

"Perhaps?" Nicholas questioned. "That response isn't good enough."

Hudson poured himself a drink. "If you don't intend to marry her, then I will."

"I don't think so," Everett muttered under his breath.

Placing the lid back on the decanter, Hudson asked, "Do you care for Madalene?"

"I do, but we're just friends."

"This sounds familiar, does it not?" Nicholas grunted.

"In what way?" Hudson asked, taking a sip of his port.

Walking over to an armchair, Nicholas sat down. "Until I admitted that I was in love with Penelope, Everett kept her tucked away at his townhouse."

"If you recall, she fled from your estate because you *ordered* her to marry you," Everett reminded him.

"It's true. I made a mistake, and I almost lost her," Nicholas agreed. "Do you intend to make the same mistake with Madalene?"

Everett sat down across from Nicholas. "We created this ruse to allow Maddie to have a Season and give her the opportunity to pick her own suitor. What kind of monster would I be if I forced her to marry me?"

"Well, I think the question that we should be asking is, do you love the girl?" Hudson inquired, looking truly curious.

"Love? No… I couldn't possibly love her," Everett stated forcefully. "We've only known each other for five days."

"That isn't unheard of," Nicholas countered.

Everett shook his head. "Putting my feelings aside, Maddie only views me as a friend."

"I disagree. I see the way she looks at you… it's rather nauseating actually." Nicholas shuddered.

Hudson nodded his agreement. "It's true. I saw the way her eyes lit up each time they landed on you."

"That's only because I saved her from Tattershell," Everett admitted sadly.

"Perhaps, or perhaps not," Hudson argued. "Regardless, you owe it to yourself to explore your feelings towards Madalene."

"What if she says no?"

"In that case," Nicholas ran his hand over his chin thoughtfully, "you can release her from the engagement with no regrets."

Everett leaned his head back and looked up at the painted ceiling. "I'm unaccustomed to being in vulnerable situations."

"Being vulnerable is the only way to find true love," Hudson remarked. "Your heart may be broken and stomped on, but isn't it worth the risk if Madalene returns your feelings?"

Everett shook his head slowly. "I don't know. Frankly, I'm scared of having a marriage like Mother and Father's."

"In what way?" Hudson asked.

Everett lifted his head and turned towards his brother. "Did you know that Father had a mistress that he kept across Town, and he had children with her?"

"He did?"

"He did," Everett repeated, taking a sip of his drink.

Hudson stared at him in disbelief. "Did Mother know?"

Everett nodded. "One day, when I came home for a holiday from Oxford, I overheard Mother crying in her bedchamber. I asked her what was wrong, and she told me that Father was leaving to visit a friend."

"A friend?" Hudson questioned.

"I followed him across Town, and I saw him entering a townhouse," Everett shared. "I went to the front window, and I saw him embracing three younger children." He huffed. "He showered affection upon them as if it was second nature to him."

Looking confounded, Hudson lowered himself onto the settee. "I had no idea that Father had another family, or that he was capable of showing any type of emotion at all."

"He deceived us all," Everett said dryly, attempting to swallow his bitterness.

Nicholas rose and helped himself to another glass of port. "What does that have to do with you and Madalene?"

"I don't want to lose her, but I'm frightened that one day, I won't be enough to keep her happy," he admitted softly.

"That's balderdash," Nicholas exclaimed. "If you truly want something, then you must be willing to fight every day for it. Fight for Madalene's love."

Everett frowned. "It's not that simple…"

"It *is* that simple," Nicholas argued, cutting him off. "Trust me."

Hudson bobbed his head. "I agree with Nicholas. Father and Mother had a marriage of convenience, whereas, you and Madalene truly care for one another. That has to count for something."

"You're both right," Everett admitted, wincing. "Starting tomorrow, I will begin wooing my fiancée."

"Excellent." Hudson bowed. "I believe my work here is done."

"Pardon?" he asked.

Hudson smirked. "Mother sent me a missive, explaining the situation and asking for my help."

Everett groaned. "And you came to flirt with my betrothed and force my hand."

"Indeed." Hudson pointed at Nicholas. "The duke was in on it, as well."

"I was," Nicholas said, rising. "Now that Everett has come to his senses, shall we join the ladies?"

Everett rose and placed a hand on Hudson's shoulder. "Don't ever flirt with Madalene again," he warned.

His brother grinned. "She's an incredible young woman. If you don't marry her, then I will pursue her."

"I'll marry her," he declared forcefully.

"See that you do," Hudson replied. "She's a woman worth keeping."

Everett nodded. "That she is."

As he watched the other two men leave the room, Everett chose to remain behind. He needed to formulate a plan to woo Maddie. But how?

13

Feeling tired and not at all excited about his upcoming visit, Everett rode the short distance to Hereford Hall. Nicholas had sent over a missive requesting that he come to call as quickly as possible.

He yawned. Again, he'd had an awful night's sleep. Every time he'd closed his eyes, he'd imagined Maddie rejecting his suit. Perhaps instead of *saying* something to her, he could deliberately prevent her from meeting any prospective suitors. That way, she would have no choice but to accept his hand at the end of the Season.

No. He couldn't do that to his Maddie. He wouldn't sabotage her chance at happiness.

When he arrived at Hereford Hall, he reined in his horse. A footman rushed down the stairs and waited as he dismounted. He removed his hat and walked up the steps. The butler greeted him as he stepped through the open door.

"Good morning, Lord Northampton," Hawkins said, then waited to receive his top hat and gloves.

"Morning," Everett muttered. "Is his grace in his study?"

The butler closed the door. "He is."

"Excellent." He took a step towards the study but then spun back around. "Has Lady…"

Hawkins cut him off with an amused look on his face. "Lady Madalene has not come down for breakfast, milord."

"Thank you," he said, tipping his head in acknowledgement.

As Everett stepped into the study, he saw Nicholas sitting at his desk, his focus on the open ledgers in front of him.

"Would you care to go riding later?" Everett asked.

Nicholas huffed. "No time." He brought his gaze up. "How do you manage to have such an enormous amount of free time to gad about London?"

"Well, I am just a lowly marquess, and you are a high and mighty duke," Everett reminded him. "And I don't gad about London."

Nicholas glanced down at a paper and wrote something. "Regardless, I think you need a pastime."

"The difference between us is that I employ a man of business and multiple stewards," Everett said. "You may want to consider relinquishing some control over your books."

"Never," Nicholas grunted.

"Well, then, perhaps you have a greater problem than managing your time, your grace," he joked.

Everett sat down in front of the desk. "Your missive was rather vague. What was so important that it couldn't wait till I came to call on Maddie?"

Nicholas placed the quill in the inkpot and gave Everett his full attention. "Mr. Swinton is set to arrive any moment. He informed me that he has some distressing news."

"Again?" Everett groaned.

"Yes, milord, again," Mr. Swinton stated as he entered the room. "This time it's about Lord Tattershell."

"Botheration," Everett mumbled under his breath.

Mr. Swinton came to stand near the desk. "Lord Tattershell has been stalking Lady Madalene."

"We are well aware of that fact," Nicholas complained. "Can you tell us something we don't already know?"

"Did you know that Lord Tattershell has gone so far as to enter your property and observe Lady Madalene's window from a distance?" Mr. Swinton pressed.

"No, I didn't," Nicholas said in a steely voice. "I want him arrested."

Mr. Swinton shook his head. "Unfortunately, no jury of his peers would convict him for trespassing."

Nicholas reached into his top drawer and pulled out a pistol. "Then, I shall just ensure Tattershell is aware that his presence is not welcome on my property."

"I would proceed with caution concerning Tattershell," Mr. Swinton advised. "He appears to be determined to continue harassing Lady Madalene."

Madalene's voice came from the doorway. "Perhaps I should start keeping a pistol in my reticule."

Everett and Nicholas rose as she walked further into the room.

Mr. Swinton bowed. "Lady Madalene, I presume?"

"You presume correctly," she replied politely. "You must pardon me for interrupting, but I heard my name mentioned as I came down for breakfast."

Coming to stand next to her, Everett provided the introductions. "This is Mr. Percy Swinton. He is the Bow Street Runner we hired to help us sort out this mess."

Madalene nodded her understanding, then faced Mr. Swinton. "Do you believe that Tattershell intends me harm?"

"I do, milady."

Everett placed a hand on the small of her back. "We won't let that happen, Maddie." He led her towards the settee.

Once she was comfortable on the settee, she pressed, "How did you become aware that Lord Tattershell was observing me from outside my window?"

"One of my men was trailing him," Mr. Swinton answered.

"I see." She turned her gaze towards Everett. "Did you not think I should have been notified that a Bow Street Runner was following Tattershell?"

"We didn't want to distress you," Everett assured her.

"By keeping me unaware of the threat on my person?" she asked, her voice rising.

Everett glanced at Nicholas for help, but he just walked over to his desk and sat down. It was evident that he wasn't going to be of any help right now.

Everett sat down next to Maddie. "Everything we're doing is to keep you safe…"

"And I thank you for that," she said, cutting him off. "But don't you think I have a right to be kept abreast of Mr. Swinton's findings?"

Sensing he was fighting a losing battle, Everett conceded. "You're right. However, we don't have much to go on right now." He shifted in his seat. "Lord Tattershell appears to be unstable after losing you. Apparently, he was relying on your dowry to restore his fortune."

"Also," Nicholas spoke up, "your uncle is apparently benefiting from your marriage to Tattershell, but we haven't discovered how."

Madalene directed her next comment to Mr. Swinton. "Have you been able to retrieve a copy of my father's will?"

He shook his head. "No, milady. You should know that your father's solicitor was found dead before your parents' funeral, and we now have reason to suspect foul play."

"I see," she murmured. "So, if I am understanding this correctly, everything depends on us finding a copy of my father's will."

"Yes, milady," Mr. Swinton confirmed.

Tilting her chin defiantly, she announced, "Then we shall

need to break into my uncle's study and see if he has kept my father's will tucked away somewhere."

"*We*?" Everett asked incredulously. "No, Nicholas and I will do the honors."

"That's preposterous," Madalene huffed. "Pray tell, what reason would you give if you were caught in my uncle's study?"

"Who said we would be caught?" Nicholas smirked.

"My uncle locks the door whenever he isn't in his residence," she shared. "Furthermore, I know which window has a broken latch and can be opened from the outside."

Everett gave her a pointed look. "You could tell us which one it is."

"I could, but I won't," she replied. "I would like to be the one that breaks into his study."

"Absolutely not," Everett declared.

She turned her attention towards Nicholas. "I used to spend hours in my father's study every day," she pressed. "I know every creak of the floorboards, and I can navigate that room in the dark."

"She does make a valid point," Nicholas conceded.

Everett clenched his jaw. "Maddie is not breaking into her uncle's estate."

"Why not? After all, if I was caught, at least I have a somewhat valid reason to be there," Madalene argued.

"And if your uncle catches you?"

"Who said that I would be caught?" She smirked.

Everett closed his eyes. "I can't ask you to do this…"

"You aren't asking. I'm offering."

"Have you even considered what your uncle would do to you if he caught you searching his study?" Everett asked.

Madalene gave him a one-shoulder shrug. "He's already banished me from my ancestral estate. What more can he do to me?"

"He could have you arrested!"

Appearing unaffected by Everett's outburst, Madalene replied calmly, "My uncle won't contact a constable for fear of inciting a scandal. Most likely, he would just kick me out of the estate again."

Mr. Swinton cleared his throat. "If I may, until we find the will, we don't know what Lord Stafford is attempting to keep hidden. He may have already killed once to keep the truth from coming out."

"Exactly," Everett replied. "It's much too risky for you."

"But not for you?" she asked, shifting in her seat to face him. "Am I supposed to just sit back and let you fight all my battles?"

Finally, she understands, he thought.

"Yes," he replied. "That's precisely what you should do."

He saw her stiffen.

"Then, you don't know me at all, Lord Northampton." She turned towards Nicholas. "I'm going to break into my uncle's study tonight while he's out gambling. Would you care to join me?"

"I would…" Nicholas started.

Everett cut him off. "If you are so insistent on going, then I shall be the one that accompanies you."

"Fine," she said, rising from her seat. "You may pick me up after the sun goes down."

He stood, took a step towards her, and lowered his voice. "You seem angry with me."

Madalene glared at him. "Of course, I'm angry with you." She pressed her lips together. "I am not some weak woman that needs to be coddled."

He placed his hand on her arm and glanced at Mr. Swinton. "Perhaps we should continue this conversation away from prying ears."

"I have nothing left to say," she declared, stepping away from him.

"But I have more to say on the matter…" His words trailed off when Madalene turned towards Mr. Swinton.

"It was nice to meet you, Mr. Swinton," Madalene said with a polite smile.

The Bow Street Runner bowed. "The pleasure was all mine, milady."

As Madalene brushed past him, Everett reached for her arm and asked, "Would you care to go on a carriage ride through Hyde Park later today?"

"Unfortunately," she answered with a frown on her lips, "I shall be much too busy embroidering."

He dropped her arm. "I shall collect you this evening then."

"Thank you," she replied before storming out of the room.

Mr. Swinton chuckled. "I like her."

Everett turned his heated gaze towards the Bow Street Runner. "Is there anything else, Mr. Swinton?" he asked in an annoyed tone.

"There is not, but you must alert me the moment you find Lord Stafford's will," the Bow Street Runner said as he departed.

Everett dropped down onto the settee. "What just happened here?" he asked.

"You somehow managed to insult Madalene," Nicholas clarified.

"But how?"

Nicholas shrugged. "I'm not entirely sure. I can ask Penelope."

"Please do," Everett said, glancing up at the ceiling. "I'm at a loss for words."

Why in blazes was Madalene mad at him for trying to protect her? It made no logical sense.

The sun was dipping over the horizon as Madalene jabbed her needle into the fabric, pulled it out, and jabbed it back in again. She was angry at Everett for attempting to coddle her. He was trying to protect her, but she was perfectly capable of sneaking into her uncle's study. Why couldn't he see that? All he saw in her was a lady needing protection.

"You're attacking that poor handkerchief quite ferociously," Penelope teased from the chair next to her.

Letting the fabric fall to her lap, Madalene huffed, loudly. "I am just so angry at Everett."

"Clearly," the duchess joked.

"Why doesn't he think I am capable of breaking into my uncle's study?"

Penelope pushed the needle into her own handkerchief fabric and gracefully pulled it out. "Our men are driven to keep us safe and protected."

"Everett is not my man."

"He is."

Madalene shook her head. "We're not truly engaged."

"And why is that?"

With a perplexed look, Madalene said, "It's just a ruse to…"

Penelope cut her off. "I'm not buying that, Maddie. You and Everett care deeply for one another."

"You're mistaken. Everett does not hold me in any affection whatsoever."

"Are you sure about that?"

Madalene nodded. "This engagement is intended to keep him from getting hounded by the *ton*'s scheming mothers."

Penelope lowered her handkerchief to her lap. "But you do care for Everett?"

Yes! Madalene wanted to shout it from the rooftops. Instead, she took a deep breath and said, "It doesn't matter what I want."

"Why not?"

Pressing her lips together, Madalene admitted, "Everett is a marquess, and he is the brother of my dear friend, Isabella. I can't be pining after him."

"What if Everett returns your feelings?"

Madalene let out a disbelieving huff. "Everett has his pick of ladies. Why would he pick me?"

"Why *not* you?" Penelope contended. "You haven't allowed yourself to let your guard down and be vulnerable, but you must if you want to be able to love without any regrets."

"Who said anything about love? I've known Everett for less than a week."

Penelope gave her a knowing look. "Falling in love is easy but staying in love requires true diligence."

"I'm not good enough for him," Madalene admitted regretfully. "Whether or not I love him will not change that fact."

"That's rubbish!"

Placing her handkerchief on the table, Madalene rose and walked to the window. "From the moment I met Everett, my life has been in shambles. I'm currently living off your charity, for heaven's sake!"

"You are not. You're my companion."

Smoothing out her blue floral cotton gown, Madalene replied, "I daresay all the clothing and accessories you bought me are worth far more than my salary."

"Regardless, you are my friend, and I don't consider you a burden," Penelope said gently.

A black coach rolled up the cobblestone drive. Everett was coming. The mere thought of seeing him brought a warm color to her cheeks and caused her heart to beat faster. She cared for him, more than she should, but that's all it could ever be. She couldn't risk getting her heart broken.

The coach came to a stop, and Everett stepped out. She took a moment to admire his dark attire, which gave him an air of intrigue.

"Perhaps you should tell Everett how you feel?" Penelope suggested, coming to stand next to her.

Madalene shook her head. "I can't. I'm not brave enough."

"Love is worth fighting for," Penelope advised.

Stepping away from the window, Madalene wrapped her arms around her waist. "What if you're wrong? What if I admit my feelings and Everett doesn't hold me in any regard?"

"Then at least you tried."

Madalene shook her head. "I won't do it. I won't risk what we have."

"And what exactly is it that you have?"

"Everett is my friend."

The butler stepped into the room and announced, "Lord Northampton is here…"

"No introduction is needed, Hawkins," Everett said as he entered.

Hawkins nodded as he slipped out the door.

An awkward silence descended over the room, broken only by the sound of the ticking floor clock.

Penelope discreetly cleared her throat. "If you will excuse me, I shall seek out Nicholas."

After Penelope slipped out of the drawing room, Everett asked, "Are you still angry with me?"

"I find that my anger has dissipated somewhat."

"Good. That bodes well for me," Everett joked as he approached her cautiously.

Keeping her face expressionless, Madalene said, "I understand you're trying to protect me, but I'm not a woman that needs to be coddled."

"I understand," he replied with a solemn expression. "From now on, I shall remember that you prefer to break into estates on your own."

Madalene found herself smiling at his teasing tone. "Thank you, but I scarcely believe this will be a common occurrence."

"What else do I need to know about you?"

She pressed her lips together in thought. "I love biscuits."

"As do I."

"I enjoy riding in the morning."

"That's the ideal time to ride. Perhaps you'll start riding astride like my sister does?"

"Heavens, no. I prefer the side saddle."

He took a step closer to her. "Shall we go riding in the morning?"

She cocked her head. "I might be persuaded."

"Excellent." He offered his arm. "Are you ready to break into Lord Stafford's study?"

"I am."

Everett led her towards the entry hall. "Mr. Swinton has confirmed that your uncle is at a gambling establishment across Town."

"That's good."

The butler opened the door as they approached. Once outside, Madalene saw three saddled geldings in the courtyard. A liveried footman held the leads.

"It would be best if we ride over to your uncle's townhouse and leave our horses with Jenkins when we arrive," he said, pointing at the footman.

She nodded her approval. "I'm glad I chose to wear one of my sturdier gowns."

Everett's eyes perused the length of her gown, and in them, she saw approval. When he looked at her that way, she felt desirable.

"You would look beautiful in a shapeless frock, my dear," he said, his voice taking on a deep, husky tone.

Madalene couldn't prevent herself from blushing, so she walked over to the gelding with a side saddle strapped to its back.

"Allow me," Everett said, helping her mount.

"Thank you," she murmured, reaching for the reins and watching as Everett mounted his horse with expert precision. His whole frame radiates masculinity, she thought.

A short time later, they reined in their horses near the back gate of her uncle's townhouse. An iron fence ran the length of the property and the darkened townhouse loomed ahead. No candlelight flickered in the windows.

Everett dismounted and came around to assist her off her horse. As he placed his hands on her waist, she leaned forward and rested her hands on his shoulders. He slowly lowered her to the ground, but he didn't release her right away. Instead, he stared deeply into her eyes.

"When this is all over, you and I are going to have a long, frank discussion." His eyes were filled with an intensity that she didn't understand.

Madalene was unable to formulate a response with Everett standing so close and looking at her that way.

A slow, smug grin tugged at his lips. "I like this more reserved side of you," he teased as he stepped back.

Ignoring his playful comment, she looked around. "The coach house and stable block are just over there. We'll need to sneak past the coachmen and grooms."

"How many does your uncle employ?"

She gave a slight shrug of her shoulders. "I know my father employed five, but I don't know if my uncle retained them."

"Understood."

Pointing at a corner window on the first floor, she said, "My uncle's study is there."

Madalene walked towards the gate and gently opened it. After she stepped through, she waited as Everett closed it with care.

Treading lightly, they remained on the paved path as they passed the coach house and stable block. Two workers chatted inside the coach house, oblivious to their presence. She headed towards her uncle's study and approached the broken window. After she opened it, Madalene turned back around to give Everett a victorious smile.

As she entered the study, her eyes scanned the large oak bookcases. Hundreds of books lined the shelves along the north wall. A large desk sitting on an ornate rug dominated the middle of the room, and a smaller writing desk sat in the corner. A portrait of her uncle hung on the east wall above the fireplace.

Madalene rushed over to the desk and lit a candle. Then, she attempted to pull out the drawers. They were locked. Drat! There had to be a key in the room, she reasoned, as she started to rummage through the items on her uncle's desk.

"Did you find anything?" Everett asked as he stood next to her.

She turned towards him and asked in a low, hushed voice, "You don't know how to pick a lock, do you?"

"I can, assuming I can borrow one of your hairpins," he replied, pointing at her head.

Madalene removed one of her long hairpins and extended it towards him. He crouched down low and shoved the hairpin into the top drawer's lock. He moved it around until it clicked.

Everett rose and pulled out the drawer. As they search through the documents, they found bills, missives from creditors, and personal notes, but they didn't discover her father's will.

Closing the drawer, Everett maneuvered the second drawer's lock in a similar fashion. They opened it and found only ledgers.

They returned the ledgers to their exact location before closing the drawer. Everett's eyes roamed the bookshelves, and he whispered, "Did your father stash any of his valuables inside of books?"

"Not that I am aware of," she admitted.

Walking up to the bookcase, Everett removed a book from a pile, causing another book to drop to the floor. They froze for a long moment.

Madalene leaned down and picked up the book. "It would appear that no one heard…" Her voice trailed off as they heard the study door being unlocked. Everett blew out the candle before he grabbed her arm and pulled her under the desk next to him.

The door to the study creaked open, and they heard booted footsteps approach the desk. The steps paused. Madalene held her breath, hoping the person would go away.

Unfortunately, she was not so lucky, because a moment later, she was staring into the barrel of a pistol.

14

Everett attempted to shift positions to place Madalene behind him, when the man holding the pistol whispered, "Lady Maddie? Is that you?"

Madalene breathed a relieved sigh. "Hayward. It's you." She crawled out from underneath the desk, and the man helped her stand. "I'm so relieved to see you."

Everett rose and dusted off his trousers.

A tall, aged man with white hair pointed the pistol at him. "Who did you bring with you?"

Madalene placed her hand on top of the pistol and pushed down gently. "This is my dear friend, Lord Northampton."

Everett frowned. Is that what she thought of him? He hoped not, because he wanted to be so much more than a dear friend.

"My apologies, milord," Hayward said, then he walked over to the door and closed it. "What are you doing in Lord Stafford's study, milady? You know no one is allowed in here when the master isn't home, for any reason."

"I know, but I'm looking for my father's will," Madalene told him.

"May I ask why?" Hayward asked as he tucked the pistol into the waistband of his trousers.

Madalene took a step closer to him. "According to my uncle, my father left me no inheritance."

"That's what he told us, as well."

"What if it was a lie?' she questioned. "I can't imagine that my father left such a generous dowry without leaving any other provisions for me."

"Could it be that your generous dowry *is* your inheritance?" Hayward asked. "After all, £30,000 would attract many worthy suitors."

Madalene nodded. "That's a good point. However, did you know that Mr. Simms was found dead the day before my parents' funeral."

The butler's eyebrows lifted nearly to his forehead. "Are you implying that Mr. Simms was murdered by Lord Stafford?"

Stepping forward, Everett said, "Not necessarily. However, don't you find it awfully convenient that the late Earl Stafford's solicitor was killed the day before the reading of the will?"

"But Lord Stafford didn't read the will after the funeral," Hayward argued, frowning.

"Exactly," Madalene stated. "Doesn't that seem odd to you?"

The butler glanced over his shoulder at the door. "What if you're wrong, and your father didn't prepare a will? I could be fired or arrested for my part in this madness."

Everett took a step closer to the butler. "If you help us, you'll always have a place in our home."

"*Our* home?" Hayward questioned, turning his gaze towards Madalene. "Are you married to this man?"

"No," she said with a shake of her head, "but we are engaged, at least for the time being."

The butler watched Madalene closely with indecision on his face. For a brief moment, Everett was sure that Hayward would refuse their request.

Finally, Hayward sighed. "Lord Stafford keeps anything of value in his safe." He stepped over to the portrait above the fireplace and lifted it down, revealing a safe inserted into the wall.

Madalene walked up to the safe and attempted to turn the handle. "It's locked."

The butler looked amused. "You didn't think your uncle would leave his safe unlocked, did you?"

She returned his smile. "It was worth a try."

Walking over to the bookshelves, Hayward ran his hand along the spines of the books until his hand stopped on one. He turned over the book and started shaking it. A key fell to the ground. He bent over, picked it up and extended it towards Madalene.

"Would you care to do the honors, Lady Maddie?" he asked.

She accepted the key and inserted it into the safe. Opening the door, she pulled out a large stack of papers, glanced back into the dark recesses of the safe, and gasped. "My mother's jewelry!"

Everett stepped forward and accepted the papers from Madalene as she turned back and began sifting through the necklaces, brooches, and rings. He placed the papers on the desk. After lighting a candle, he sorted through the pages until he found it. The late Lord Stafford's will.

"Madalene, I found it," he declared in a hushed but urgent voice.

Holding it close to the candlelight, he started reading. After a moment, he froze.

"What's wrong?" Madalene asked, coming to read over his shoulder.

He turned to face her. "Under your father's will, you are entitled to £40,000, Benham Manor, and the surrounding lands. You were also given certain pieces from your mother's jewelry."

Reaching for the papers in his hand, Madalene took a moment to read for herself. "I was entitled to my inheritance on my eighteenth birthday," she read. "Lord Stafford wasn't even supposed to be my guardian. It was supposed to be my second cousin, Lady Frampton."

Hayward spoke up. "I overheard Lord Stafford discussing Benham Manor with his solicitor. He plans to put it up for auction."

"He can't sell my mother's ancestral home!" Madalene exclaimed.

Everett bobbed his head. "Agreed. We need to get this will to my solicitor, because I have no doubt that Lord Stafford will claim it's a forgery."

"Most likely, it will go to court," Hayward admitted.

Madalene grinned. "It's a good thing I know a prominent barrister to represent us."

"I see nothing funny about this, young lady," Hayward huffed, but there was no anger behind it.

Tucking the will into his jacket pocket, Everett picked up the other papers and placed them back into the safe. He closed and locked it before extending the key back towards Hayward.

"Thank you for helping us," Everett said gratefully.

"It was my pleasure," Hayward replied, accepting the key. He deposited it back into the book and returned it to its proper place. "Normally, I would suggest you exit through the main door, but I don't want your presence known."

Madalene embraced her butler. "I've missed you," she whispered fondly.

Hayward brought his arms around her. "I've been so worried about you. Lord Stafford hasn't mentioned you once since he returned from the garden party."

"That's because I ran away. I am residing at the Duke of Blackbourne's townhouse."

"The Duke of Blackbourne, you say," the butler repeated. "He is a good ally to have, milady." He glanced over at Everett. "How exactly did you become engaged to Lord Northampton?"

Madalene smiled kindly. "That's a long story, and one that we don't have time for now. I promise to tell you everything as soon as I can."

Hayward returned her smile. "Have courage, Lady Maddie." His words were spoken with affection, clearly speaking to the bond they shared.

"Thank you," she murmured. "I shall return after we have sorted out this mess."

"I look forward to it," he replied.

Everett reached for Madalene's right hand and started leading her towards the window. "It's best if we don't dally too long."

"I agree," Madalene replied before she exited.

As Everett bent to duck out the window after her, Hayward's voice stopped him. "Take care of our Maddie," he said with a hint of an edge in his tone.

"You have my word as a gentleman," Everett responded.

Hayward tipped his head in acknowledgement.

Once they were both through the window, they hurried with light steps towards the trees where Jenkins guarded their horses.

Everett knew what he held in his pocket changed everything. Madalene was an heiress in her own right. Once she realized that she didn't need to marry for money, would she still honor their agreement?

Sitting at the head of the table for breakfast, Nicholas asked in disbelief, "He dropped a book?"

Madalene nodded in amusement. "I had managed to sneak us past the stables and into my uncle's study, but Everett picked up a book from the bookshelf and caused them all to come cascading down."

"I see you are prone to exaggeration, my dear," Everett sighed. "It was only one book."

Reaching over, Madalene patted his sleeve. "Lucky for us, it only alerted my family's butler, Mr. Hayward."

"Who offered to help us, might I add," Everett remarked. "Without him, we would have never discovered the will." He gave her a smug smile. "You could even say that I saved the day by dropping that book."

"I would hardly go that far," she bantered.

Penelope wiped her mouth with a white napkin. "I can scarcely believe that your father left you £40,000, an estate and land, and your uncle never intended to let you lay claim to any of it."

"I knew my uncle was an unsavory man, but I had no idea he would stoop so low as to cheat me out of my own inheritance," Madalene admitted.

Everett reached for his teacup. "My brother has agreed to meet with us later today. Furthermore, I directed my man of business to copy the will and deliver it to Hudson's office prior to our meeting."

"That was clever of you," Madalene said.

"Dear heavens, *woman*, are you flirting with me again?" he asked, mock disbelief in his tone.

"Of course not." She feigned shock, then laughed. "I was merely stating a fact."

Nicholas groaned. "Don't puff up his ego any more. Everett is barely tolerable, as it is."

Reaching for her cup of chocolate, Madalene asked, "Would either of you care to join us for a ride through Hyde Park?"

"Sadly, I cannot. My cousin, Baldwin, is coming to go over the company books," Penelope replied.

"And I have work to do," Nicholas grumbled.

After taking a sip, Madalene directed her next comment to Penelope. "I can't believe you're running your own company."

"I'm grateful to be surrounded by like-minded individuals who have come to accept the fact that I am only a lowly woman with an inferior intellect," Penelope joked wryly.

Nicholas reached out and tenderly encompassed his wife's hand. "Don't let my wife fool you. She's already surpassed last year's profits because of her effective management."

"I, for one, knew you had it in you, Penelope," Everett said, raising his teacup.

"Thank you, Everett," Penelope murmured before turning her loving gaze back towards her husband.

Everett leaned closer to Madalene. "Are you finished with your breakfast?"

Reaching for the last piece of bacon on her plate, she quickly ate it, then said, "I am now."

"Good," he replied, rising from his seat. "I know it's not a fashionable time to ride through Hyde Park, but you mentioned that you prefer to ride in the morning."

"I do."

"There's a pond on the north side of Hyde Park that I thought you might enjoy. The trail leading up to it has trees on both sides."

"That sounds divine."

Accepting Everett's offered hand, she took a moment to enjoy the sensation of his skin against hers as he helped her rise. He tucked her hand into the crook of his arm before leading her outside.

"How does it feel to be an heiress?" he asked as they approached the stables.

A bright smile came to her face. "It feels invigorating," she admitted. "I won't be forced to rely on the charity of others."

"No one is helping you begrudgingly, Maddie," he replied, giving her a pointed look.

"True, but I feel a sense of freedom knowing that I have the funds to take care of myself."

He nodded. "That's a wonderful feeling."

They arrived at the stable, and Madalene admired two already-saddled geldings waiting for them. She walked up to the horse with a side saddle.

"Allow me," Everett said as he intertwined his fingers and held them down for her to step on.

Madalene placed her foot into his hands, and he gave her a boost up onto her horse. Then Everett mounted, and they turned towards Hyde Park. After they raced through the fields, they slowed their horses to a walk, and she admired the trees lining their path.

"Be honest with me," Everett started in a serious tone, "are you thinking about climbing one of those trees?"

She grinned. "I am, but I only climb trees when no one else is around."

"Smart girl."

Madalene caught a glimpse of sparkling water up ahead, and Everett veered his horse towards the pond. "We should give our horses a chance to drink."

"I concur," she said, following him to the pond.

Everett dismounted and walked over to assist her. After her feet were on the ground, he stepped back, creating more than enough distance to be considered proper.

"Have you considered what you intend to do next?" he asked, watching her closely.

"Vaguely," she admitted. "I had briefly considered visiting Benham Manor."

"You would leave Town in the middle of the Season?"

Reaching down, she picked up a smooth rock. "It's just one possibility." She flicked the stone over the water and was gratified to see it skip three times before dropping in.

"What about us?" he asked in an earnest voice.

"Us?" she repeated. "There is no *us*, Everett. We aren't truly engaged."

A pained expression crossed his face. "Regardless, we had a deal. We would stay engaged till the end of the Season. I'm surprised that you would renege on our deal so easily."

"No, Everett," she rushed to reassure him. "I didn't realize you felt so strongly about this."

"Well, I do," he said, his voice rising.

Madalene shifted her gaze back towards the pond. "I'm sorry for upsetting you. I won't go to Benham Manor till the end of the Season."

Everett breathed a deep, heartfelt sigh. "Frankly, I don't want you to leave at all."

"What exactly are you saying, Everett?" she asked, looking back at him.

Moving deliberately, he came to stand in front of her. His steady gaze met hers, and his blue eyes held her transfixed.

"I would like to change the terms of our agreement."

She stilled, holding her breath. "Meaning?"

Everett's gaze intensified. "I want to turn this arrangement into…"

"Get down… *now*!" a man shouted from somewhere in the trees.

Everett grabbed her arm and pulled her to the ground just as the sound of a pistol discharging came from the woods. She heard a bullet whizzing above her head.

"We need to get you out of here!" Everett ordered. "I'm going to put you on your horse, and I don't want you to stop riding until you arrive at Hereford Hall."

"What about you?" she asked urgently.

"Don't worry about me. I'll be right behind you." He rose and lifted her onto the horse in one swift motion. "Stay low and ride."

She was about to kick her horse into a run when she heard another shot ring out. This time, it was followed by Everett grunting in pain.

Glancing down, she saw him crouching down on the ground, holding his chest. Blood stained his white shirt and waistcoat. Without hesitating, she slid off her horse and rushed to his side.

"What are you doing?" he asked through clenched teeth.

"I'm saving you. What do you think I'm doing?" She grabbed his right arm and helped him up. "We need to get you on your horse."

Everett's breathing became labored, and he hissed, "Save yourself, Maddie."

"I think not," she argued as she slowly led him towards his horse.

Everett was leaning heavily on her, and she had no idea how she was going to get him into the saddle.

Unexpectedly, a tall man with dark hair ran out of the bushes and approached them. "Allow me, Lady Madalene," he said as he came to stand next to Everett.

She relinquished her spot even as Everett shouted in protest, "No, you have to help Lady Madalene get to safety first."

"That's nonsense, Everett," she declared from behind them.

"I'll help Lady Madalene as soon as you are atop your horse, milord," the stranger stated.

Madalene noticed how Everett was now leaning most of his weight on the man. Feeling frightened and relieved at the same time, she looked at the fellow who'd come to their aid.

"Thank you," she said. "I don't know how I would have gotten him on the horse without your help. May I ask who you are, and how you know my name?"

"I'm the man the Bow Street Runners assigned to follow Lord Tattershell." His words were rushed as he helped Everett onto his horse.

Once Everett was mounted, he reached for the reins and ordered, "Now help Lady Madalene."

"As you wish," the man replied. Without asking permission,

he scooped her up and placed her on her side saddle. "Now run, and don't stop until you're far away from here."

She waited until Everett kicked his horse into a run before she followed suit. As they raced away from the pond, she heard another pistol being discharged in the woods. Lucky for them, they appeared to be out of range.

Who was shooting at them? And why?

15

"You're cheating," Madalene declared as she tossed her cards onto the table. "No one can be this good at piquet."

Everett chuckled. "You're an exceptionally sore loser."

"You've won the last five hands in a row," she complained as she collected the cards. "Would you like to play again?"

Shaking his head, he placed his right hand over hers. "It wouldn't be right for me to beat you again."

With a sour face, she snatched her hand back. "Before your winning streak, I did beat you three times."

Everett gave her a look of pity. "That's what losers say, my dear."

Her green eyes lit up, brightening her beautiful face. "I'm glad to see you're feeling better," she replied as she divided the cards into two piles.

Wincing in pain as he shifted in his chair, he said, "I was fortunate that the bullet just grazed my chest and only required a few sutures."

Madalene started shuffling the cards. "Which one of us do you think the person was shooting at?"

"I don't know," he replied honestly.

"We believe you were the target, Lord Northampton," Mr. Swinton said, walking swiftly into the room with Nicholas following close behind.

Everett attempted to sit up in his seat, but a jolt of pain went through his chest, and he reluctantly relaxed against the back again. "Who was the shooter?"

Mr. Swinton's eyes darted between him and Madalene. "It was Lord Tattershell. He was waiting in the woods to ambush you."

"I want him arrested!" Everett growled with such ferocity that Madalene jumped in her seat.

"We're working on that, milord," Mr. Swinton reported, "but he's vanished."

"How could he just vanish?" Everett asked, lowering the intensity of his voice.

Mr. Swinton frowned. "After you two rode away, my man tried to detain him, but Tattershell shot him in the leg."

"Is your man all right?" Madalene asked.

Mr. Swinton nodded. "Yes, but he's in the hospital."

Placing his hand over his own wound, Everett inquired, "Was he the man that saved us?"

"Aye, Lord Northampton," Mr. Swinton replied. "He saw what Tattershell intended to do, and he tried to warn you."

"I would like to give that man a £100 bonus for his bravery," Everett pledged.

"That's awfully kind of you," Mr. Swinton said sincerely.

"Nonsense. He saved my life, but more importantly, he saved Madalene," Everett stated. "It's the least I can do."

Madalene placed the shuffled cards to the side of the table. "How do you suppose Lord Tattershell knew we were going to be at that pond?"

"My man informed me that he was standing outside the dining room this morning while you were discussing your plans," Mr. Swinton explained.

"Again, Mr. Swinton, why was Tattershell not taken into custody for trespassing on my property?" Nicholas demanded.

"As I've mentioned before, it's nearly impossible to convict a member of the peerage," Mr. Swinton replied. "Even if we have irrefutable proof, a man in his position could still be acquitted, even for manslaughter."

Everett shifted in his seat and grunted a bit at the pain. "He shot at me… three times. I truly believe he intended to kill me."

"As do I, which is why I have issued an arrest warrant for attempted murder," Mr. Swinton asserted. "Let's pray a jury of his peers won't acquit him for intentionally shooting at the Marquess of Northampton."

"Good," Everett muttered. "I want to see him hang."

Mr. Swinton shook his head. "At most, he'll be fined and ordered to stay away from you and Lady Madalene."

"He won't go to jail?" Madalene asked, shocked.

"No, milady. Since this is his first offense, Lord Tattershell can claim privilege of peerage to escape punishment."

Madalene clasped her hands in her lap. "That's terrible."

"It is," Mr. Swinton agreed.

"Why was Tattershell shooting at Everett, do you suppose?" Nicholas asked.

With a solemn expression, Mr. Swinton replied, "Most likely for revenge. Furthermore, I urge you to use caution when you go about your daily business, milord. He's out there somewhere, and he intends to do you harm."

"I understand," Everett responded. "As a precaution, I would like a Bow Street Runner to be assigned to Lady Madalene."

"As you wish," Mr. Swinton said. He disappeared from the room without another word.

Everett glanced over at the floor clock. It was nearly time to meet his brother. With a bit of difficulty, he rose. "We must make haste if we want to meet Hudson on time."

"Do you think that's wise, considering your condition?" Madalene asked, her concern evident in her tone.

"My condition?" he repeated.

She glanced down at his chest. "Your injury, I mean."

"I'm perfectly able to step into a coach and allow myself to be driven to my brother's office across Town," Everett remarked dryly.

"That may be true. However, it might be best if Nicholas and Penelope were to accompany me to the meeting with your brother, while you stay here and rest."

"Do you think I'm some kind of invalid?" he questioned, feeling offended.

She shook her head. "No, but I *am* worried about you."

Her obvious concern dissipated his anger. "I'm fine, Maddie," he reassured her. "I'd like to be the one that accompanies you to the meeting."

"I'll order the barouche to be brought up front," Nicholas said, "and I'll ensure your lady's maid travels with you for propriety's sake."

"Thank you, Nicholas," Madalene replied with a smile.

The duke's face softened at the use of his name. He nodded his acknowledgement and departed from the room.

Madalene stood up and walked over to Everett. She placed her hand on his forehead. After a moment, she muttered, "No fever." She almost sounded disappointed.

"Stop fussing over me, *woman*," he ordered, trying to sound stern despite feeling pleased at her abundant show of compassion. Maybe she did hold him in some high regard?

Crouching down next to his chair, her glistening eyes met his.

"What's wrong?" he asked.

She bit her lower lip before she answered. "I've never been so scared in my life." Her voice softened, so he had to strain to hear her. "I almost lost you."

"It's all right." Reaching over, he lightly traced her high cheekbones with his fingers. "It's going to take more than a bullet to stop me from being with you."

Blinking back tears, she replied, "I am so incredibly sorry for bringing Lord Tattershell's wrath upon you. I wish he'd been shooting at me. After all, I'm the one who deserves it."

"That's not true," Everett contended. "Besides, I can deal with Tattershell, but I could never cope with losing you."

She smiled, albeit a small one. "You've saved me twice now."

"No. I daresay that you saved me this time," he murmured. "You could have ridden off, but instead you jumped off your horse and came to assist me."

"I couldn't very well leave you!" she exclaimed, sounding shocked at the very idea.

Everett's fingers began to trace the line of her jaw and the rounded curve of her chin. "You should have."

"I would have never left you alone." Her words were soft and tender.

His voice hitched as he whispered, "Today, you were *my* hero."

"We're even then?" she breathed.

"No, I will forever be in your debt."

"Why?"

He paused as he heard Nicholas's voice come from the doorway. "Yes, why?"

Leaning back, Everett asked in an annoyed tone, "Have you been eavesdropping this entire time?"

"I have," Nicholas said unrepentantly. "After all, this is my townhouse."

"Blast him," Everett muttered under his breath.

Nicholas stepped further into the room. "Language, Everett. A lady is present."

Laughing, Madalene rose and stepped away from him. "Allow me to go and collect my gloves."

Once Madalene left the room, Nicholas said, "I thought you were going to offer for her."

"I already did offer for her, and she said yes," Everett reminded him.

"Yes, but now you want to offer for her because you love her, not just to keep desperate young ladies and their scheming mothers away."

Everett arched an eyebrow. "What is it with you and Penelope about love?"

Shrugging, Nicholas replied, "I suppose we want everyone to be as ridiculously happy as we are."

Everett glanced at the door. "I was about to confess my feelings earlier by the pond, but Tattershell started shooting."

"I strongly encourage you to offer for Madalene again before word of her inheritance spreads among the *ton*. Between her dowry and her inheritance, she'll be highly sought after, even if she is already engaged."

"You're right," Everett said with a bob of his head.

"Of course, I'm right. I'm always right." Nicholas stepped closer to him and lowered his voice. "Do you need assistance into the barouche?"

With an exasperated sigh, Everett rose and walked out of the room. He was not an invalid. He was perfectly capable of riding in a barouche. But at that moment, a stabbing pain shot across his chest.

Sitting next to her lady's maid in the barouche, Madalene politely nodded as Amy spoke at her usual fast pace. She saw Everett attempting to stifle a smile as he sat across from her.

"I've never ridden in a barouche before," Amy shared, her eyes lighting up with excitement. "This one is so fancy. I feel like a proper lady."

"This is one of the grander barouches I have ridden in," Madelene admitted.

Amy giggled. "The bench is so plush that it would be heavenly to nap on." She took a breath before continuing. "Can you imagine taking a nap in a barouche? What a silly thought."

"Indeed," Madalene replied, amused by Amy's excitement.

"There's so much traffic on the roads today," Amy remarked.

Everett spoke up. "That's because the streets are narrow, and the foot paths are congested. Many times, the street sellers inadvertently block the roadways with their carts and stalls."

"My sister is a street seller," Amy revealed, still watching the traffic.

"I didn't realize that. What does she sell?" Madalene asked.

"Freshly baked bread," Amy responded. "She sets her cart up on the foot paths near Ackermann's Repository, and she makes more money than me." Her hand flew to cover her mouth as she gasped. "I apologize if I sound ungrateful, milady. I assure you that I am most grateful for everything the Duke and Duchess of Blackbourne have given me."

Madalene smiled reassuringly. "Not at all. I can hear how proud you are of your sister's accomplishments."

Amy let out a loud sigh of relief. "It's true. You're most gracious. I can't believe your uncle is trying to deny you your inheritance. He's a loathsome man." Her eyes widened. "Again, I'm sorry. I should never have said that."

"It's all right, Amy," Madalene replied. "I agree with you. My uncle *is* a horrid man."

The coach came to a stop outside of a large, white-washed brick building, and a footman came around to open the door. Everett exited first and placed his right hand out to assist her. Madalene was grateful for his steady hand as she stepped down onto the narrow, slippery pavement. Hordes of pedestrians lined the foot paths, and they all appeared to be in a rush to get to their various destinations.

When Everett reached out to assist Amy from the barouche, she tentatively placed her hand in his and stepped out onto the pavement.

Once her feet were on the ground, Amy clasped her hands in front of her as she stared at the building. "How exciting! I've never been to Old Bailey before." She looked at Madalene. "Mrs. Seymour informed me that I am supposed to walk behind you and sit outside the door while you're in your meeting."

"You're welcome to walk next to us," Madalene encouraged.

"Heavens, no!" Amy exclaimed. "I wouldn't want to anger Mrs. Seymour, now would I?"

"Of course not," Madalene agreed as Everett offered his right arm to her. Her eyes scanned the various street sellers, wondering if one was, perhaps, Amy's sister. "Why are so many people on the pavement today?"

"Modiste and millinery shops line these streets. It's inevitable that pedestrians would be trapped by admirers examining the latest fashions displayed in the shops' windows," Everett explained.

"I don't blame the ladies for stopping to look at the latest fashions," Madalene remarked as her foot slipped on the slick pavement. She gripped Everett's arm tighter, and she could feel taunt muscles underneath his jacket.

"Careful. It rained earlier, and that can create slippery passageways," he warned.

Everett led her past a brick wall forming a semi-circle in front of the stately building. He tipped his hat at the guard stationed near the wall, then, opening the door of the Old Bailey, he stepped aside to let the ladies enter first.

"The courtroom is on the first level, and Hudson's office is on the second level," he informed her.

"It's quite impressive that his office is in the Old Bailey," Madalene commented.

Everett's voice reflected pride as he shared, "My brother was just appointed as a district judge."

"That's wonderful news," she gushed.

As they stepped inside the foyer of Old Bailey, Madalene saw a large crowd assembled, their clothing befitting their differing economic stations.

Everett leaned closer to her and whispered, "These men and women paid admission to sit in the gallery to watch the courtroom proceedings."

"Fascinating," she murmured. She had to admit that it would be rather interesting to watch a case being tried.

A large set of stairs led up to the second level, and they proceeded down a narrow hall. When they arrived at Hudson's office, Everett pounded on the door with his fist.

It was opened, revealing Hudson with a smile on his face. "Welcome, Brother." He turned his gaze towards her. "It's a pleasure to see you again, Lady Madalene." Gone was his flirtatious nature, replaced with a much more respectful tone.

"Likewise, Lord Hudson," she replied with a smile.

Opening the door wide, he invited them in. "Welcome to my office."

Everett gestured that she should go first. As she stepped into the office, she noted the fireplace with a mosaic on the front and a large Turkish carpet in the center of the room. A mahogany desk sat in front of the lone window overlooking the Old Bailey courtyard and chairs lined the walls.

"Your office is exquisite, Lord Hudson," she said politely.

Hudson's eyes swept over the room with pride. "I agree."

Walking further into the room, Everett placed a hand on his brother's shoulder. "I'm proud of you, Brother."

"Thank you, but you may want to save your praise until after our meeting with Lord Stafford," he warned, coming around his desk.

Madalene stilled. "We're meeting with my uncle?"

Hudson nodded as he sat down. "After reading the will, it was quite evident that it's in Lord Stafford's best interest to honor the will before this case goes to trial and ruins his good name."

"Does Lord Stafford have a good name?" Madalene asked incredulously.

"As questionable as that may be," Hudson hedged, "I'm hoping those words will convince him to cooperate with us. I've invited Lord Stafford's solicitor to attend the meeting, as well." He glanced over at Everett. "Do you have the signed will on you?"

"I do," Everett said, reaching into his pocket and removing several folded sheets of paper.

Hudson accepted the papers, and his eyes scanned the document, lingering on the signature and the red-crested wax seal. "There's no reason to doubt the authenticity of this document."

Madalene breathed a sigh of relief. "That's wonderful news."

"But we can't proceed until Lord Stafford arrives and states his argument," Hudson responded, placing the papers on the desk. "Have you retained a solicitor yet?"

She shook her head. "I have not."

"Normally, you would hire a solicitor first, and then a barrister would be hired when the case goes to trial," Hudson stated. "However, I'm glad that you came to me first. I am appalled by Lord Stafford's deceit."

A knock came at the door. Everett stood and answered it, revealing Lord Stafford and a man wearing thick spectacles.

Lord Stafford's eyes narrowed as he stepped into the room. "What are Lord Northampton and my niece doing at this meeting?"

Hudson rose from his desk. "I have assembled everyone

together to hopefully bring this case to a satisfactory resolution for both parties without having to go to trial."

Pushing the spectacles up on his nose, the other man walked in and introduced himself. "My name is Mr. Ezra Cooke, and I represent Lord Stafford."

"Excellent," Hudson said, pointing towards one of the chairs sitting off to the side. "If you will both sit down, we can begin this meeting."

Once Madalene sat down, all the men in the room followed suit.

"As you may be aware, I am a district judge, and a former barrister," Hudson began. "My brother, Lord Northampton, asked me to assist him on this rather distasteful matter."

Lord Stafford humphed but remained silent.

"I've reviewed the will of the late Earl of Stafford, Mr. Ralph Ramsbury, and I have found it to be authentic," Hudson reported in a solemn tone.

"That's ridiculous!" Lord Stafford shouted. "My brother didn't leave a will."

"According to Lady Madalene, she found it in the safe in your own study," Hudson stated matter-of-factly.

Lord Stafford jumped up from his seat. "That's outlandish! I demand my niece be arrested at once for trespassing."

"You have that right," Hudson admitted, "however, I would discourage that course of action, especially since your niece has the right to sue you civilly for your deceit."

"There's no deceit! Whatever document that she claims to be her father's will is a forgery," he insisted, but Madalene thought she detected a hint of uncertainty in his eyes.

Hudson reached for the will and held up the last page with her father's signature and crested wax seal. "I've analyzed Lord Stafford's signature, and it appears authentic. However, we can bring in an expert to confirm the authenticity of the will, if you desire."

"Do that," Lord Stafford said with a wave of his hand.

"While we wait for an amicable resolution to this matter, it is my recommendation that Madalene be given an income to pay for her living expenses," Hudson said calmly.

Lord Stafford's eyebrows shot up. "You want me to give a monthly stipend to my niece?"

"Your treatment of your niece has been deplorable at best, and I have no doubt that the judges will rule in her favor," Hudson stated in an authoritative voice. "I would even consider your actions criminal, Lord Stafford, and I would urge the Crown to prosecute you for your deception."

Mr. Cooke put his hands up in front of him. "This has all been an unfortunate misunderstanding. My client is adamant that the will in front of you is a forgery and not from his deceased brother."

"Have you had a chance to review the will?" Hudson asked, extending the papers towards Mr. Cooke.

The solicitor rose and accepted them. As he reviewed the pages, his frown intensified. He leaned over and whispered something to Lord Stafford.

"Absolutely not," her uncle seethed.

Mr. Cooke again whispered something to his client.

This time, Lord Stafford nodded his acknowledgement.

Extending the will back to Hudson, Mr. Cooke said, "Lord Stafford still maintains that the will is a forgery. However, he has graciously agreed to provide Lady Madalene with an income during the time it takes an expert to review the document and confirm its authenticity." He turned his gaze towards Lady Madalene. "We believe a sum of £10 a month is fair."

"I think not," Everett huffed.

Hudson gave his brother a pointed look before turning his gaze back towards Mr. Cooke. "I think a more reasonable sum would be £100 a month."

"£100? Are you mad?" Lord Stafford exclaimed.

"Of course, all the income that she receives would be deducted from her inheritance," Hudson clarified.

Mr. Cooke leaned over and whispered something to Lord Stafford, causing him to shake his head vehemently.

Frowning, Mr. Cooke acknowledged, "Lord Stafford is willing to a compromise of £20."

Hudson rose from his chair. "I've heard enough. I will direct Lady Madalene to hire a solicitor, and I will personally represent her in the court's proceedings."

"You?" Lord Stafford scoffed.

"As I stated previously, I was formerly a barrister, and I have an impressive record of winning," Hudson said, his tone confident. "We intend to pursue criminal charges against Lord Stafford for his complete and utter disregard for Lady Madalene's well-being."

"Wait, that's not necessary," Mr. Cooke insisted. "If you file charges, it could damage Lord Stafford's reputation."

"Lord Stafford's own selfish actions have intentionally damaged Lady Madalene's reputation by forcing her into an engagement with Lord Tattershell," Hudson replied simply. "Quite frankly, I care more about restoring Lady Madalene's good name than trying to protect Lord Stafford's questionable one."

"I would like a moment to confer with my client," Mr. Cooke said, stepping to the door. He opened it and waited for Lord Stafford to exit the room.

As soon as the door was shut, Lady Madalene heard her uncle and his solicitor having a loud, heated discussion, but she couldn't distinguish any words. Finally, silence prevailed. Then Mr. Cooke opened the door with a frown.

Lord Stafford walked back into the room with his arms crossed defiantly.

Mr. Cooke spoke up. "Lord Stafford is willing to release Benham Manor to Lady Madalene and the specified pieces of her mother's jewelry, but he is unable to give her any additional funds."

"And why is that, Lord Stafford?" Hudson asked the earl directly.

Lord Stafford's lips curled in disdain. "Running two estates is expensive, and I was forced to dip into the reserves to pay for the maintenance.

"How much of Lady Madalene's inheritance is left?" Hudson pressed.

Her uncle uncrossed his arms. "None."

Madalene's eyes widened and Everett choked, but kept silent.

Hudson kept his face expressionless. "None?"

"I'm broke, which is why I was planning to auction off Benham Manor to raise additional funds," Lord Stafford admitted.

Picking up the will, Hudson reviewed the document, then said, "When this will was drafted four months prior to Lord Stafford's death, as his heir, *you* were entitled to £100,000 in funds, several parcels of land, two country estates, and a London townhouse."

"What's your point, barrister?" Lord Stafford growled.

Hudson dropped the papers to the desk. "I recommend you sell your entailed properties, Lord Stafford, and pay your niece the £40,000 inheritance that you owe her."

"If I do that, I'll be ruined," her uncle argued.

"That is of your own making," Hudson pointed out, "and that is not your niece's concern."

Lord Stafford turned his attention towards her. "Be reasonable, Madalene. Running multiple estates is expensive, and you don't want me to have to fire all the household staff because of your greed."

"*My* greed?" Madalene rose slowly. "You attempted to force me into a marriage with Lord Tattershell and tried to rob me of my inheritance to save yourself from your own financial ruin! You cared not one whit for my reputation or well-being!"

"You were a fool not to marry Lord Tattershell," he mumbled.

"You are a horrible, despicable man!" she declared.

Lord Stafford snarled. "That money and property should have been mine. I am the Earl of Stafford, and you are just a woman."

Everett opened his mouth to respond, but she put a hand on his sleeve, stilling his words. He realized that this was her fight, and she was more than ready for battle.

Madalene took a step closer to him. "I'm sorry you feel that way, Uncle, but you're wrong. My father willed me that money because he loved me, and he wanted to see me provided for."

"What are you going to spend all that money on?" Lord Stafford asked. "Gowns, accessories, and other frivolous items?"

"No." Madalene shook her head. "I'm going to live my life and be who I am meant to be."

"You have no concept of how expensive it is to run an estate," Lord Stafford stated.

"You're right, but I have no problem asking for help."

Lord Stafford's eyes narrowed, and he took a step closer, bringing him within arm's length of her. "You've always been an impertinent thing. You should be thanking me for taking you in after your parents' death."

"About that," Hudson interrupted, "you were never appointed Lady Madalene's guardian. That honor belonged to Lady Frampton."

"That senile old bat?" Lord Stafford questioned with amusement. "You wouldn't have lasted three days at her country estate in Scotland."

"I wouldn't know, now would I?" Madalene remarked cheekily. "I was denied that privilege because of your deceit."

Her uncle brought his hand back to slap her, but she remained rooted to her spot, unyielding.

"I would think twice about striking me," she warned firmly. "I plan to follow Lord Hudson's advice and pursue criminal and civil charges against you. Striking me here, in front of witnesses, certainly won't help your case."

Lowering his hand, Lord Stafford glared at her. "You wouldn't dare. It would bring scandal to our family's good name."

"Our family's good name was ruined the moment you inherited the earldom."

Her uncle's eyes radiated hate at her. He spun around and left the room without saying another word, slamming the door behind him.

Mr. Cooke pushed his spectacles further up on his nose. "Perhaps we can avoid going to trial by reaching a settlement, assuming Lord Stafford is willing to sell the entailed properties."

"I may be amenable to that plan," Madalene stated.

Lord Stafford's solicitor nodded and left the room.

Coming to stand next to her, Everett smiled proudly. "Well done, Maddie."

"I must agree with my brother," Hudson said. "You stood up to Lord Stafford and came out the victor."

She directed her next question to Hudson. "In your opinion, will I ever see that money?"

"Unfortunately, you may only receive a small settlement after his other creditors have been paid," he explained with a small wince. "If it helps, I have no doubt that we will win the civil and criminal cases against your uncle."

"That does ease my mind," she expressed. "What I don't understand is how my uncle was not able to spend my dowry?"

Picking up the papers on his desk, Hudson explained, "As stated in your father's will, your dowry was set aside in a separate account that could only be accessed *after* you were married."

"Then, how would my uncle have benefited from my marriage to Lord Tattershell?"

"I haven't figured that out yet." Hudson shook his head. "Lord Stafford truly believed no one would discover his deceit."

Everett huffed. "Stafford is a cocky, brash man."

"That he is," Madalene agreed before turning her attention back to Hudson. "I cannot thank you enough for what you've done for me today."

Hudson grinned. "You are most kindly welcome, but perhaps you should wait to thank me until after the court proceedings are over."

"Are you ready to depart, Maddie?" Everett asked, extending his arm towards her.

"I am," Madalene replied, placing her hand in the crook of his arm.

As Everett led her out the door, she felt drained. Her uncle had most likely gambled her inheritance away. What a cruel twist of fate to discover she had inherited £40,000 only to discover she would never be able to lay claim to it.

At least she had Benham Manor. Perhaps the estate would produce an income large enough for her to survive. Keeping her head held high, Madalene walked out of the Old Bailey, ignoring Everett's concerned glances, and stepped into the waiting barouche.

Once they were situated, Amy asked excitedly, "How did the meeting go?"

Madalene blinked back her tears. "Not well."

"It'll all work out, you'll see," Amy encouraged.

Madalene closed her eyes and leaned her head back against the plush bench. Right now, she just needed a moment to sort out her feelings.

16

Dressed in a white muslin gown, Madalene idly pushed the food around her plate as she listened to Penelope, Nicholas, and Everett conversing politely around the dining table. She wasn't hungry, and she wanted to be alone, but somehow Penelope had managed to coax her out of her room for supper.

Madalene's thoughts kept returning to the meeting with her uncle. With her newfound inheritance, she shouldn't be forced to marry this Season. She should be able to retire to Benham Manor and managed the estate. However, she had no funds to pay for its upkeep. Was there even staff still at the manor, or had her uncle already fired them? A panicked thought came to her mind. What did she know about hiring staff?

Penelope's voice broke through her musings. "Oh dear, I think we've lost her."

"Again?" Nicholas asked from the head of the table.

Everett joked, "She must have tired of hearing Nicholas's war stories."

"Impossible," Nicholas objected. "No one tires of hearing those."

"That's true," Penelope replied with tenderness in her voice. Reaching over, she placed her hand on Madalene's arm. "Maddie, dear. Are you with us?"

"My apologies." Madalene brought her head up with an apologetic smile. "I'm afraid I was woolgathering."

"Are you thinking about your uncle again?" Everett asked knowingly.

She nodded. "I was wondering if he had fired the staff at Benham Manor in anticipation of the auction."

"It would have been logical to do so," Penelope responded.

Putting her fork down, Madalene admitted, "If so, I don't know anything about hiring staff. I wouldn't even know where to start!"

Penelope smiled kindly at her. "Don't fret. We'll contact our solicitor in the morning, and he can handle all the particulars."

"I'm tired of everyone fighting my battles for me," Madalene said with a sigh. "This is *my* mess, and I should sort it out on my own."

Everett watched her closely. "You don't have to go about this all alone, Maddie."

"I know, but everyone has already done so much for me. I don't wish to be a burden anymore," Madalene admitted, feeling her eyes fill with unwanted tears.

"Who said you were a burden?" Penelope asked, arching an eyebrow. "You've been an excellent companion."

Madalene huffed. "I have done little by way of being your companion."

"That's your opinion," Penelope contended. "As your employer, I'm quite satisfied with your performance of those duties."

Madalene's shoulders slumped. "Finding out about my inheritance was the first time that I felt like I could finally take care of myself. Yet here I am, continuing to rely on your charity."

Everett shoved back his chair. "Would you care to take a turn around the garden, my dear?"

Madalene glanced out the darkened window, and it was on the tip of her tongue to refuse. However, when she saw Everett's hopeful expression, she knew she couldn't deny his request.

"Very well," she said as a footman came to pull out her chair.

Everett came around the table and offered his arm. "We shall return shortly for a rousing game of whist," he announced over his shoulder, directing his comment to Penelope and Nicholas.

Madalene and Everett walked out the rear door of the townhouse and step down into the well-manicured gardens.

Everett glanced over at her. "Are you finished feeling sorry for yourself?"

She dropped her hand from his, frowning. "You have no right to speak to me in such a way."

"I have no right?" he asked, turning to face her. "You have been moping around since we left Hudson's office."

"Of course I have!" she declared. "My uncle gambled away my inheritance."

"You still have Benham Manor. That's more than most people have."

Madalene's frown deepened. "Pray tell, since I have no funds, how can I pay for the upkeep of the estate and household staff?"

"You may be pleasantly surprised to discover the estate produces an income."

"Perhaps," she mumbled. "But will it be enough?"

"Well, you could sell it."

She glanced up, looking a bit shocked. "I would prefer not to."

Everett took a step closer. "Look around you, Maddie. You're not alone in the world. You have Penelope, Nicholas, and me."

Her eyes turned towards Hereford Hall. "And what if Penelope and Nicholas tire of helping me?"

"Then you have me," he asserted, placing his hands on her shoulders. "You will *always* have me."

She shook her head. "No, I won't. At the end of the Season, we shall go our separate ways."

"That was our original plan, but is that what you want now?"

Pressing her lips together, Madalene replied, "It doesn't matter what I want."

"It doesn't?" Everett cocked his head. "What if we posted the banns and were married at the end of the Season?"

"No," she said, shrugging out of his hold. "I will not force you into a marriage you don't really want."

Everett watched her with an intense expression. "Who said anything about being forced? Who says I don't really want to marry you?"

Madalene took a step back, attempting to create more distance between them. "No. The whole point of this ruse was for you *not* to be forced into an unwanted marriage."

"That's true, but things have changed between us."

Wrapping her arms around her waist, Madalene fought the tears threatening to fall. "Why would you want to marry me, Everett? After all, you could have your pick of any woman in Society."

"That's true," he remarked smugly. "But no other woman is *you*." He started to take a step closer, but she placed a hand on his chest to stop him.

"Your mind is muddled from the events of today," she insisted. "You only want to marry me to protect me."

"That's not true," he contended.

She opened her mouth to respond but stopped when she heard a thump. She stifled a scream as Everett groaned and dropped to his hands and knees, his head hanging down. Behind him stood Lord Tattershell, holding a pistol in his hand.

"Madalene, dear," Lord Tattershell greeted in a devilish voice, "we meet again."

"Run, Maddie," Everett ordered, still not raising his head.

Madalene's blood ran cold as she saw blood trickle down the side of Everett's face from the gash on the back of his head.

Rearing back his foot, Lord Tattershell kicked Everett in the stomach.

Everett grunted loudly as he doubled up and his head dropped even lower.

"I tire of your useless chatter, Northampton," Lord Tattershell whined. "If it wasn't for you, Madalene and I would already be wed. This is all *your* fault." He reared back and kicked him again.

"Stop!" Madalene cried. "It isn't his fault; it's my fault! *I* was the one that ran away."

"But he gave you the opportunity," Lord Tattershell sneered.

Dropping down next to Everett, she pleaded, "Leave him be… please."

"I'm afraid I can't do that."

"Why not?"

Lord Tattershell cocked his pistol and pointed it at Everett's back. "Because I intend to leave no witnesses."

Throwing herself onto Everett's back, she cried, "Don't hurt him."

"And why shouldn't I?"

"Because if you don't harm him, I will come willingly," Madalene promised.

Lord Tattershell eyed her suspiciously. "You would willingly come with me?"

"No, Maddie," Everett groaned. "Save yourself."

Ignoring him, she continued to press her case to Lord Tattershell. "Yes, and you need not fear Everett. He's still weak from when you shot him earlier, so he won't be able to follow us."

A rustling noise came from the brush, and her eyes darted in that direction. If she was lucky, it would be the Bow Street Runner assigned to protect her.

Lord Tattershell let out a low, harsh laugh. "If you are hoping for a Bow Street Runner to assist you, then you will be sorely disappointed. I already killed the one that's been trailing me."

"How could you be so cruel?" she asked, fear filling her voice.

"Cruel?" He shook his head. "No, my dear, I'm just taking back what's mine."

She tilted her head defiantly. "I am not yours."

"You are," he said in a firm tone. "Now get up."

"Not without your word that you won't hurt Everett," she replied just as firmly.

He reached down and grabbed her arm. "I said '*get up*'," he ordered as he yanked her to her feet.

Everett finally raised his head and looked up at Lord Tattershell. "You won't get away with this," he said, pain in his voice.

"You see, I already have," Lord Tattershell replied in a matter-of-fact tone. "Once I marry Madalene, my fortune will be restored."

Lord Tattershell pointed the pistol at Everett again, and Madalene saw his finger twitch on the trigger. He intended to shoot her fiancé, and she refused to let that happen.

"No!" She reached for the barrel of the pistol, shoving it into the air just as it discharged. Ignoring the burning sensation in her hand, she reached under Everett's arm and attempted to lift him up. "Run, Everett!"

"I won't leave you," he stated as he tried to stand.

She pulled at his arm again. "You have to."

"What have you done, you foolish chit?" Lord Tattershell growled as shouting came from the direction of Hereford Hall. He gripped her arm tightly and shoved her towards the cover of the trees.

"Madalene!" Everett shouted as he tried to rise on the paved pathway.

As she fought Tattershell's iron grip, Madalene attempted to wriggle out of his clutches. He stopped once they cleared the trees and seethed, "You have left me no choice."

He gripped the pistol in his hand and slammed it against her cheek. The last thing she remembered was being tossed over his shoulder. Then, everything went black.

"Where in the blazes is Mr. Swinton?" Everett grumbled as he paced the floor in Nicholas's study.

"You need to calm yourself," Nicholas urged as he stood near the drink cart with a snifter in his hand. "Come get something to drink."

Everett shook his head, and he immediately regretted that movement as it began to throb. To make matters worse, he felt stabbing pain where the doctor had sewn up the gash on the back of his head.

Penelope walked into the room. "You should be resting, Everett."

"Not until I have Madalene safely back in my arms," he declared as he stepped to the drink cart and poured himself a drink. "I don't know why we're waiting for Mr. Swinton when we should be out searching for Madalene."

"Pray tell, where would you look?" Nicholas asked. "We don't even know if Tattershell was riding in a coach or on a horse."

Wincing in pain, Everett took a sip of his drink. "It was evident that he plans to take her to Gretna Greens."

"If that's true, then there are countless roads he could have taken to avoid detection," Nicholas pressed. "I've learned over the years that you may lose the battle, but you can still win the war."

"Enough of your military examples," Everett growled.

"All right, how about this piece of advice," Nicholas said sternly. "You're injured, and you'll do Madalene no good if you go off half-cocked searching for her."

A man's voice came from the doorway. "His grace is right, Lord Northampton."

Turning towards the door, Everett saw Mr. Swinton walk further into the room.

"Do you know where Madalene is?" Everett asked.

Mr. Swinton nodded. "I do."

"Where?"

"Curtis was assigned to watch over Lady Madalene, and he paid a man to report her location to me. She's at a public house known as The Beehive in Epping Green parish near the town of Hertford."

Everett gripped the drink in his hand tightly. "May I ask why this Curtis fellow didn't intervene when Tattershell was abducting Madalene?"

"While Curtis was in the woodlands watching over Lady Madalene, he spotted two men fighting in the brush. He approached them and saw Tattershell standing over Dowding with a bloody dagger in his hand. Tattershell turned and left, so Beaumont raced to try and save Dowding's life. When he heard the pistol discharge, he stopped and immediately made his way towards the gardens. That's when he saw Tattershell riding away with Lady Madalene on his lap.

Placing his glass down on the drink tray, Everett said, "I am sorry for the loss of your man."

"Thank you. Tattershell has killed one of my men, and he will be charged with murder once we arrest him.

"Good. My only regret is that he can only be hung once," Everett declared, storming towards the door.

"Wait!" Mr. Swinton shouted after him. "You should know that Tattershell isn't alone. He has two guards with him."

"I want to hire every available Bow Street Runner, and we will storm The Beehive," Everett declared.

"If we do that, then Lady Madalene might be injured in the ambush, milord," Mr. Swinton pointed out. "I propose you let us handle this matter."

"Absolutely not. I hired you to keep Madalene safe and to keep an eye on Tattershell. We both know how that went," Everett replied dryly.

Mr. Swinton frowned. "Now is not the time to lay blame. We must retrieve Lady Madalene, and time is of the essence."

"You're right," he admitted. "Regardless, I'm going with you."

Penelope spoke up. "You're injured, Everett. You need to rest."

"Not until Madalene is safe," Everett insisted.

Walking over to his desk, Nicholas pulled a pistol out of the top drawer and tucked it into the waistband of his trousers. "I'm going as well."

"Of course, your grace," Mr. Swinton replied. "It would be my privilege to fight alongside you."

Nicholas stepped over to Penelope and kissed her soundly on the lips. "Don't worry, my dear. We'll bring back Madalene safely."

"Do you have an extra pistol?" Everett asked.

Nicholas considered him for a moment. "I'm not sure that's a good idea."

"Why not?"

Frowning, the duke pointed to Everett's head. "You're injured."

Everett lifted his brow. "Your point?"

"We all want to bring Madalene back home," Nicholas started, "and it might be best…"

Everett cut him off. "I *am* going," he declared forcefully. "I intend to bring home my betrothed."

"Did Madalene accept your suit?" Penelope asked curiously.

He shook his head. "No. We were interrupted, *again*, by Tattershell."

"If you hadn't been interrupted, do you think she would have said yes?" Penelope pressed.

"I don't know," he admitted. "She keeps saying that she doesn't want to force me into an unwanted marriage."

Penelope walked closer to him. "Have you told her that you love her?"

"No…" Everett turned away from Penelope's knowing gaze and admitted, "I didn't."

"Next time you see Madalene, you must let her know *why* you want to marry her," Penelope advised.

Everett bobbed his head. "I can do that." Then, he corrected himself. "I *will* do that."

"Good, because women like it when men confess their feelings," Penelope shared.

"It's true," Nicholas agreed as he retrieved a pistol from behind a book on the bookshelf. "That's how I won Penelope over." He extended the weapon towards Everett. "Don't do anything foolish, Everett."

"I can't promise anything," Everett stated honestly as he reached for the gun.

Nicholas sighed. "That's what I'm worried about."

"I will do whatever it takes to get Madalene back," Everett declared. "I can't lose her."

"And you won't," Nicholas replied. "Just try not to get yourself killed."

Mr. Swinton started walking towards the door. "I asked your butler to prepare your horses. If we run them all the way, we can arrive at the public house within an hour."

Nicholas turned back towards Everett. "Are you sure you want to join us?"

"I certainly do!" Everett exclaimed.

Nicholas's eyes grew determined. "It will be dangerous."

"I have no doubt."

"Then, let's go save Madalene… together."

17

Madalene awoke with a jolt as Tattershell reined in his horse. They stopped in front of a brick building. A streetlamp stood outside of the business, illuminating the cobblestone courtyard and a sign above the door, which read The Beehive.

"Ah, good," Lord Tattershell said, looking down at her. "You're finally awake. For a moment, I was worried that I hit you too hard."

She brought her hand up to her cheek and felt dried blood caked on her skin. Lord Tattershell shifted in the saddle, and she realized that she was sitting on his lap. Immediately, she tried to create some distance, but he slid his arm around her waist, holding her in place.

"Allow me to dismount first," he ordered.

Once he was on the ground, he reached up and grabbed her waist, yanking her forward. He released her when her feet were on solid ground.

Two men reined in their horses in the cobblestone courtyard beside them.

"No sign we were followed, milord," the red-headed one announced.

"That's good," Lord Tattershell replied. "It's much too dark to be on the roads any longer. We shall rest and resume our journey early tomorrow."

The men dismounted as a lanky young man exited the public house. "Can I get yer horses, misters?"

"You may," Lord Tattershell said. "I want my horse to be brushed down and fed generously." He reached into the pocket of his waistcoat, pulled out a few coins, and extended them towards the young man.

The young man's eyes lit up with excitement.

"Thank you, sir," he gushed. "Your horse will be well cared for."

Lord Tattershell nodded approvingly before offering his arm to her.

Madalene stared at his proffered arm, but she made no move to accept it.

"You will behave, my pet," he growled.

She lifted her brow. "I will not."

Unexpectedly, Lord Tattershell reared back and slapped her hard across the face.

"You will *not* defy me," he commanded.

"I will *never* stop fighting you," she replied, ignoring the throbbing in her cheek.

"Let me make one thing clear, my dear." His eyes narrowed as he removed the pistol from the waistband of his trousers. "If you run from me, I will kill you."

"I thought you needed me alive," she challenged, trying to control her sudden trembling.

Lord Tattershell stepped closer to her and trailed the barrel of the gun down the side of her face.

"Only until we marry, then your usefulness will be over."

Madalene swallowed slowly and was grateful when he took a step back.

"Now," he began, "let's try this again." He extended his arm towards her, and she obediently placed her hand over his.

"That's better," he crooned as he tucked his pistol back into his trousers.

Lord Tattershell led her into the public house, where loud, boisterous noise floated out of the hall. The smell of freshly-baked bread floated in the air, but it was mingled with the strong smell of ale.

A stout man with a little grey around his beard and temples broke through the crowd and approached them. "What can I do fer you folks?"

"We need two rooms and a private room to dine in," Lord Tattershell replied.

The innkeeper's gaze fixed on her cheek, and she saw the disapproval in his eyes. But rather than attempt to assist her, his eyes traveled back to Lord Tattershell. "We can do that, sir. Follow me."

The innkeeper walked across the main room, skirting men that were clearly inebriated. He opened the door to a side room where she saw a writing table, a small table with four chairs, and a brick fireplace in the corner.

"Will this do, sir?" he asked.

Lord Tattershell shoved her into the room. "It will." He turned back towards the innkeeper and extended him some coins. "Bring us food and ale."

"As you wish," the innkeeper said with a slight nod before departing.

Madalene stepped around the table to create more distance between her and her captor.

Lord Tattershell pointed at her. "This is all your fault, you know."

"In what way?"

He pulled out a chair and sat down. "If you hadn't run away, then I wouldn't have had to use such harsh tactics with you."

She noticed a brass handle poker resting against the fireplace. Perhaps I could use that as a weapon, she thought briefly.

"I hadn't realized what a feisty thing you were," Tattershell said condescendingly, then he chuckled. "I see you're considering arming yourself with a dull poker."

"I will not marry you," she asserted, turning her attention back to him.

"You will," he stated matter-of-factly.

She shook her head. "I would rather die."

"That can be arranged, my pet," he growled, shoving back his chair.

Shuddering at his venomous tone, Madalene shifted her gaze towards the floor. How was she going to get out of this tangled mess?

Lord Tattershell's booted footsteps echoed in the small room as he approached her. He stopped in front of her and waited until she looked up at him. He brought his hand up and ran his finger along her bruised cheek.

"You see, my dear, your uncle lost you in a game of cards."

"I was not his to lose."

"Shhh… little one." He pressed his finger against her lips to silence her. "At first, I didn't want to shackle myself with a wife, but then he explained that you came with a £30,000 dowry."

"After beating your uncle, I had a string of bad luck and ultimately lost everything." His beady eyes roamed over her face, then he licked his chapped bottom lip as he focused on her mouth. "That's why I had to marry you. If not, I would have been thrown into Marshalsea Prison."

"What if I just gave you the money?" she asked hopefully. "Or, I can give you Benham Manor."

"No." He shook his head. "Now, I want you, as well."

Without warning, he wrapped his arm around her waist and

pulled her close to him. Crushing his lips to hers, his kiss was hard, unyielding. She fought valiantly against him, refusing to let him deepen the kiss. She pushed away from him as hard as she could, then slammed her heel down on his Hessian boot.

He spewed a string of curse words as he leaned back, but he did not release her.

"I see you'll need a bit more convincing."

"I will never be yours," Madalene hissed as she swiped at her mouth with her hand, attempting to remove the feel of his lips on hers.

"Oh, my shrew," he said with a dry chuckle. "You'll be fun to tame."

A knock came at the door before a young serving girl with blonde hair dressed in a clean, but faded, blue dress walked into the room with a tray of bread, cheese, and four bowls of soup. She placed it in the center of the table, then asked, "Will there be anything else, sir?"

Lord Tattershell glanced at the open door. "The gentlemen that I came with…" His voice trailed off as loud laughter came from the main hall.

"Yes," the girl replied, nodding. "They stopped at the card table, sir."

"Card table?" Lord Tattershell asked, his eyes gleaming with interest.

"It's just outside of this door," the girl informed him.

Lord Tattershell released Madalene and stepped outside of the room.

The serving girl's eyes met Madalene's with an imploring look. She nodded at the tray and whispered, "There is paper under the tray."

Madalene nodded her understanding and shifted her gaze to the floor when Lord Tattershell re-entered. The serving girl curtsied and left without saying another word.

Walking closer to the table, Lord Tattershell sat down and

reached for a spoon. He quickly ate the soup and a few pieces of bread without speaking to her. Then, he shoved the bowl away and rose.

"I'm going to be right outside this door," he announced. "If you try to escape, I will break your legs."

Her eyes widened at his threat, knowing he meant every word.

"I understand," she replied in a submissive voice.

"Good." Lord Tattershell nodded in approval. He crossed to the door, opened it, and slammed it behind him.

Immediately, she rushed to the table and found two pieces of paper under the tray. She stepped to the writing desk and reached for a quill. After dipping it into the ink pot, she wrote:

"I have been abducted by a mad man. I will reward you handsomely if you help me!"

MADALENE FOLDED the paper and placed it back under the tray. She then took the second paper and placed it in front of her on the writing table. She knew there was a chance that she might not come out of this situation alive. She intended to fight Lord Tattershell until her dying breath. She knew Everett deserved to know the truth if it came to that. She dipped the quill into the inkpot and wrote:

MY DEAREST EVERETT,

Please know that I love you, and my heart belongs to you. No matter what happens with Tattershell, that will never change. You are my hero, and always will be. Just know, if I die, that as I drew my last breath, I was thinking of you.

. . .

All my love,
Maddie

She folded the note and addressed it to Everett. Then, she slipped it into the pocket of her gown. The door opened with a creak, and the serving girl stepped into the room.

"Are you finished, miss?" she asked, glancing down at the tray.

"Yes," Madalene replied with a nod. "I'm afraid I'm not very hungry."

The serving girl reached under the tray, removed the piece of paper, and slipped it into her apron pocket.

"Perhaps you'd like me to leave the tray, in case your appetite returns?"

"Very well," Madalene said with a smile. "Thank you."

Madalene watched as the serving girl left the room, closing the door behind her. She turned towards the darkened window. What if she climbed out the window? She sighed and banished that thought. Even if she managed to escape, she was unfamiliar with this town and wouldn't even know where to hide.

She stepped over to the table and ripped off a chunk of bread. As she chewed, she heard the window being slowly pushed open. She turned her head and saw the serving girl peering inside.

"We must get you to the constable," the girl whispered.

"Where does the constable live?" Madalene whispered back as relief washed over her.

"On the other side of town," the girl replied, stepping away from the window. "My father is distracting those men, but you don't have much time."

Madalene hurried and climbed through the opening. Once

her feet landed on the ground, she felt her slippers sink into the mud.

"Follow me," the serving girl whispered as she quietly closed the window.

They'd just made it the short distance to the main road when she heard Lord Tattershell shout, "Madalene!"

The girl grabbed her arm and pulled her towards the trees surrounding the town. "You hide, and I'll go get the constable."

As she escaped into the safety of the trees, Madalene kept running deeper and deeper into the woods. She refused to stop, because she knew what her fate would be if Lord Tattershell found her.

Everett leaned low in the saddle as they raced their horses towards The Beehive. He had never felt such raw, uncontrollable hatred for someone as he did for Tattershell. Not only had the man ambushed him twice, but he had taken the most important thing in his life, Maddie.

Maddie was his. Once this was all over, and she was safely back in his arms, he would confess his undying love to her.

A brick building with a slate roof came into view, and they reined in their horses near the entrance to the public house. A short man with dark hair stepped out from the shadows.

"You made good time," he said.

"Is she still inside, Curtis?" Mr. Swinton asked as all the men dismounted.

"Aye," he replied. "Last I checked, the three men were playing cards in the corner."

The door to the public house opened, and a young boy ran out to collect their horses.

Everett removed a gold coin from his waistcoat pocket, and

he extended it towards the young man. "Stand watch over our horses. We may need to make a hasty retreat."

"Yes, sir," the young man said excitedly as he accepted the coin.

Nicholas removed the pistol that was tucked into his trousers and strode purposefully towards the door. He opened it wide, and his commanding presence immediately filled the room. A hush descended over the hall, and every man in the room turned to look at him.

Nicholas stepped further into the room, and a stout man approached him. "I'm the keeper of this inn. May I help you, sir?"

"I'm looking for three men, and a lady wearing a white gown," Nicholas said as his eyes scanned the room.

"What do you want with the lady?" a brawny, red-headed man asked as he rose from a table in the corner.

"It's none of your concern," Nicholas remarked dismissively.

"It's my business now." The man retrieved a pistol from the back of his trousers. "Why don't you turn around and leave quietly?"

Nicholas's face was unreadable as he turned to face the man. "I will not. I've come to bring the lady home."

"You shall go home empty-handed or dead, mate." The man smirked as another man rose from the same table, holding a pistol in his hand, as well. The second man wasn't as brawny as the first, but he was still husky.

"I'm not your *mate*," Nicholas remarked dryly. "You should probably count before you make threats. After all, there are four of us and only two of you."

"I was a sharpshooter for the Royal Army," the brawny man replied smugly.

"You still only have one shot," Nicholas pointed out.

"One is all I need," he responded, his tone turning hard.

Holding his gun in his right hand, Everett came to stand next to his friend as the other patrons darted for cover.

Nicholas lifted his brow. "I'm surprised you don't have a double-barrel flintlock like mine."

A hint of fear entered the brawny man's eyes, but he blinked it away.

"That doesn't matter," he boasted. "Once I kill you, I'll strip you of your pistol."

"You're a fool," Nicholas said. "Put down your pistol, and you can walk out of here alive."

The man huffed. "What makes you think you can order me around?"

"Allow me to introduce myself," Nicholas replied in a strong, authoritative voice. "My name is Nicholas, and I am the Duke of Blackbourne."

The husky man's mouth gaped as he stared at Nicholas in awe. Slowly, he lowered his pistol to the table and stepped to the side.

"You coward," the brawny man hissed.

"I will not shoot his grace," the man whispered back. "I heard he killed a hundred French soldiers with his bare hands."

"That can't possibly be true," the brawny man argued, his eyes darting towards Nicholas. "Can it?"

Nicholas clenched his jaw. "I tire of this useless chatter. Draw your weapon or stand down."

In the next moment, the brawny man brought up his gun, and Nicholas discharged his pistol, hitting him directly in the chest.

As the brawny man dropped to the floor, Nicholas turned back towards the innkeeper and asked, "Where is the lady?"

The stout innkeeper frowned at the dead man. "After seeing the blood on her cheek, and the fine quality of her garment, I knew she was in a precarious position," he replied. "My daughter helped her climb out the window, but the man discovered she was missing only moments after she escaped."

"Where are they now?" Everett asked.

"My wife saw the lady running towards the trees while my daughter raced to Constable Hill's house," he explained.

"Show us," Nicholas ordered.

"Yes, your grace," the innkeeper replied with a nod. "Follow me."

He led them through the main entrance and around back. As they followed closely behind him, Everett's eyes scanned the woods, looking for any sign of Madalene.

The innkeeper stopped next to a hornbeam tree with moss covering its branches. "She ran that way, and the man was not far behind."

Nicholas took control of the situation. "Fan out and search for Lady Madalene. If you see Tattershell, kill him or apprehend him, I don't truly care which. We just need to keep Madalene safe."

"The woodlands are quite treacherous," the innkeeper warned. "The land is on a gentle downwards slope, but moss covers the ground, making it quite slippery. Furthermore, you must be careful of the low hanging branches."

"Thank you," Everett replied with a nod. "We'll be all right."

Mr. Swinton spoke up. "Will you ensure that the constable is aware that the Duke of Blackbourne, the Marquess of Northampton, and two Bow Street Runners are searching these woods for Lord Tattershell?"

The innkeeper's eyes widened as he stared at the gentlemen. "Yes, I will see to it."

Without another word, Nicholas darted to the right of the tree and entered into the dense woods. Everett ran straight ahead, being careful of the roots sticking up from the ground.

As he hurried through the trees, using only the moonlight to light his path, his eyes kept scanning the woodlands, hoping for some sign of Madalene. Suddenly, he saw a flash of white up ahead.

The occasional sound of an owl hooting in the distance was all he heard as he slowed and crept closer to that flash of white. A bird took flight from a tree near him, startling him. His heart began to beat rapidly as he gripped his pistol tighter.

Out of nowhere, a rock came flying at him and hit him in the chest. He grunted loudly as he doubled over. He barely had time to catch his breath before another rock hit him in the forehead. Quickly, he darted behind a tree. He brought his hand up to his forehead and felt blood trickling down the bridge of his nose.

Tentatively, he peered out from behind the tree to look for his assailant, but he saw no one. The woods were eerily calm.

Suddenly, a thought occurred to him. Maddie wouldn't be hiding on the ground. She would have climbed a tree and remained silent. He decided to change tactics.

Cupping his hands around his mouth, he called in a hushed voice, "Maddie." He turned his head in the other direction and said her name again. "Maddie."

"Everett?" Madalene's hesitant voice came from above.

"Where are you?" he asked as his eyes turned upward, scanning the trees.

"I'm up here," she replied, before she started climbing down from a large beech tree.

Once her feet were on the ground, Madalene ran towards him, jumping into his arms.

"You came for me!" she cried, tightening her hold on him.

Ignoring the pain radiating in his chest, he murmured into her hair as he held her close, "Always."

"I'm sorry I threw rocks at you," she said as she leaned back. "I thought you were Lord Tattershell."

"Rocks are still preferable to bullets." He smiled gently.

"Lord Tattershell is somewhere in these woods," she shared with a furrowed brow. "I've heard him shout my name multiple times."

Everett saw the worry in her eyes. He wanted to wipe away

her pain, to bring back the joy and contentment that usually graced her face. His hand traced the gash on her cheek, and he saw her wince.

"He hit me so hard with his pistol that he knocked me unconscious," she revealed softly.

Everett tensed. "No one will ever hurt you again."

Madalene nodded, and the look in her eyes was unmistakable. She trusted him completely.

"Do you know how to get out of these woods?" she asked.

"I have a fairly good guess," he replied, stepping back and reaching for her hand.

Lord Tattershell's voice came from behind him. "Well, apparently, I have no choice but to kill you, Northampton."

Slowly turning around, Everett gently pushed Madalene behind him.

"I don't think so," he replied.

"Step away from the chit," Tattershell ordered as he stepped out from the shadows of the trees, his pistol pointing at Everett.

"I will not," Everett answered loudly, hoping to alert the others.

"Tell me, Northampton," Tattershell said, walking closer to them and keeping his pistol trained at Everett's chest. "I have shot you, hit you with my pistol, and yet, you won't give up. Why is that?"

"Because Madalene is mine," Everett proclaimed.

Lord Tattershell tsked. "No, she's mine. Her uncle gave her to me." He cocked the pistol. "Now you shall die, and that will give me great pleasure."

"No!" Madalene shouted as she tried to step in front of him, but Everett put his arm out to stop her.

"Tell *me*, Tattershell," Everett said, "have you paused to consider that perhaps I didn't come alone?"

"No bother," Lord Tattershell stated with a shrug of his

shoulder. "As I've already demonstrated, Bow Street Runners are no match for me."

"That may be," Everett paused, "but what of the Duke of Blackbourne?"

Lord Tattershell scoffed. "I can defeat a duke."

"Can you?" Everett asked. "After all, he is a war hero."

Everett heard the cocking of a pistol behind Lord Tattershell.

"I daresay that a *child* could best you, Tattershell," Nicholas taunted.

"Look who decided to join the festivities," Tattershell mocked, his pistol wavering.

Nicholas's tone turned thunderous. "Drop your gun, or I will kill you right here."

"As you wish." Lord Tattershell lowered his weapon to the ground, but as he started to straighten, he retrieved a dagger from his boot.

Before Everett could warn him, two more pistols were cocked in the night.

"Drop the knife, or you're a dead man," Mr. Swinton warned from the shadows.

Pursing his lips, Tattershell dropped the dagger onto the moss-covered ground. "I was only claiming what was mine," he whined.

"No," Mr. Swinton replied as he stepped out from behind a tree. "You murdered a Bow Street Runner and tried to kill the Marquess of Northampton."

"He tried to kill me *multiple* times," Everett pointed out.

Tattershell huffed. "I'm a member of the peerage. Laws don't apply to me."

In one swift motion, the duke hit Tattershell over the head with the side of his pistol and watched as the man crumbled to the ground.

"I grew tired of hearing his voice," Nicholas remarked,

turning to direct his next comment to Mr. Swinton. "I shall ensure he hangs for his crimes."

"Thank you, your grace."

Nicholas gave him a curt nod.

"Shall we go home?" Everett asked Madalene.

"That sounds wonderful," Madalene replied with a sigh of relief.

When she moved to stand next to him, Everett slipped his arm around her shoulder and tugged her close.

"Will you be all right sharing a horse with me?" he asked.

She gave him a brief smile. "I will be."

"You're safe now, I promise."

"I know," she sighed. "Thank you for saving me… again."

"That's what I do, save people," he teased.

Nicholas groaned. "That was awful, Everett. If I recall, I was forced to save *you*, as well."

"I had everything in hand," Everett announced boldly.

"Did you now?" Nicholas asked, clearly not believing him.

"I did," Everett replied with a nod. "But you intervened before I was able to carry out my plan."

"You are an imbecile," Nicholas replied with a shake of his head.

"Perhaps we can continue this conversation on the way back to Hereford Hall," Madalene suggested, laughing. That sound warmed Everett's heart.

"Good idea, my lady," Everett replied, offering his arm.

Madalene accepted it and smiled over at him.

As he guided them out of the trees, he felt a sense of pure contentment enter his heart. His Maddie was safe and back in his arms. Now he just had to convince her to stay there forever.

18

As Everett hurried up the steps of Hereford Hall, he had an extra bounce in his step. He was eager to see how Madalene was faring after he'd left her in Penelope's care late last night.

He'd barely slept a wink. He couldn't stop thinking about what he intended to say to convince Maddie to marry him. He knew she cared for him, but she didn't seem to believe his intentions were pure. Well, he would win her over!

The door opened, and the butler stepped to the side, allowing him to enter.

"Morning, Lord Northampton."

"Morning, Hawkins," he said, stepping into the entry hall. "Has Lady Madalene come down for breakfast?"

"I'm afraid not."

Everett attempted to hide his disappointment. That was not the answer he'd been hoping for. "Is his grace in his study?"

"Yes, milord."

As he stepped further into the entry hall, Everett heard Madalene's lady's maid call his name from the top of the stairs.

He stopped and waited as she quickly descended the stairs. He stifled a smile. The poor girl walked as fast as she talked.

"Yes, Amy," he answered, pleased with himself for remembering her name.

"This note was addressed to you," Amy said as she extended a folded piece of paper towards him.

"Who is it from?"

"From my mistress, Lady Madalene," she revealed. "It was in her dress pocket."

Everett unfolded the note and read the words. He felt his heart leap for joy. More importantly, he felt victorious! Not only did Lady Madalene hold him in high regard, but he had earned her love as well.

Bringing his gaze back towards Amy, he asked, "Did Lady Madalene ask you to deliver this note to me?"

"Oh!" Amy's eyes grew wide. "I didn't ask her. I assumed because your name was on it… When I saw you riding up, I…"

"It's all right," Everett interrupted her. "I'm glad that you gave me the note."

Amy let out a sigh of relief. "That's good. I was worried that I'd done something wrong."

"No, what you did was wonderful," he replied with a smile.

"Very good, milord." Amy curtsied, then returned up the stairs.

Tucking the note into his blue jacket pocket, Everett couldn't believe his good fortune. Madalene loved him! True, she'd written the note under duress, but he believed she truly meant those words. Now, he just had to confess his love, and they would live happily ever after. He was sure of it.

As he continued to walk down the hall to Nicholas's study, he saw Madalene walking towards him. She was wearing the most alluring pale-yellow gown with a square neckline. Her hair was piled high on her head and curls framed her face.

"Morning," he greeted.

"Morning." She offered him a cheery smile, despite the large bruise and cut on her cheek.

He didn't stop until he was in front of her. "How did you sleep?"

"Very well. And you?"

"Quite soundly." His eyes roamed over her face. "Did it hurt when the doctor sewed up your cheek?"

"It did," she replied as she gently touched them. "But I'm sure it hurt no worse than when *you* received stitches on the back of your head or on your chest."

"Good point, my lady," he said, watching her. Should he confess his feelings now and be done with it?

She eyed him with concern as she dropped her hand. "Are you feeling all right? You look rather confused at the moment."

He chuckled. "Is that a bad thing?"

"I haven't decided yet," she answered, pursing her delicate lips. "I suppose that depends on what you're confused about."

Offering his arm, he decided to change the subject. "May I escort you to breakfast?"

"You may," she replied, placing her hand on his arm. "I find myself famished this morning."

"Well, in that case, I hope there's plenty of bacon for you."

She grinned. "I do love bacon."

"I know. Every morning you pile the bacon onto your plate." He smiled down at her. "I've made it my personal mission to learn everything about you."

"Is that so?"

"Yes, after all, you are still my betrothed."

Her grin disappeared, and she stared straight ahead. "I believe I made my intentions clear last night, Everett. I refuse to force you into marriage."

"You were perfectly clear," he said, "but things have changed."

"Have they?" she asked, glancing over at him.

"Yes," he replied, "and I'm beginning to think I'm winning you over."

She shifted her gaze away from him. "I have no interest in being in a marriage of convenience, no matter how charming you may be."

"You think I am charming?" He smirked.

"*Every* lady thinks you are charming," she replied defensively.

He stopped and turned to face her. "I'm not talking about other women. I'm asking you. Do *you* think I am charming?"

Madalene pressed her lips together for a moment, then revealed, "Yes, I do. Happy?"

"I am," he replied as he turned to resume their walk across the entry hall.

A knock came at the main door, and Hawkins opened it, revealing Everett's brother.

"Hudson?" Everett asked. What was his brother doing at Hereford Hall?

Hudson removed his black top hat as he entered. "I was hoping you would be here when I called upon Lady Madalene."

"Why are you calling on Lady Madalene?" Everett asked through clenched teeth.

Hudson grinned. "Not for the reason you're thinking." He bowed towards Madalene. "How are you faring this morning?"

"Very well," she responded with a curtsy.

"I've received wonderful news, and I wanted to come straightaway to tell you," Hudson shared.

"Come, let us adjourn to Nicholas's study," Everett said.

As they stepped into the study, the duke rose from his desk. "Hudson, it's good to see you this morning."

"Likewise, your grace," Hudson greeted with a bow. "I've come to share some good news with Lady Madalene."

Nicholas gave Madalene a curious look. "Would you like me to step out, Lady Madalene?"

"No," she replied with a shake of her head. "Whatever news Lord Hudson has come to deliver, you are more than welcome to hear."

Everett led Madalene to a camelback settee and waited until she sat down, then claimed the seat next to her.

Hudson stood in front of them and announced, "Lord Tattershell has been charged with murder, attempted murder, kidnapping, and a bevy of other charges. The evidence has mounted against him, and I have no doubt that he will hang for his crimes."

"That's terrific news!" Everett exclaimed.

"I also have some rather unfortunate news," Hudson said with a frown. "I was informed this morning that the high court has opted *not* to charge Lord Stafford with the murder of Mr. Simms."

"Did they state why?" Everett asked.

Hudson's brow furrowed. "According to their report, Mr. Simms was known to do business with some rather unscrupulous people on the docks, and they don't believe there is enough proof to get a conviction."

"Is that true?" Madalene questioned.

"I suspect not," Hudson replied, shaking his head, "but it's nearly impossible to convict a member of the peerage."

"What?!" Madalene cast him a look of disbelief. "So, my uncle may get away with the murder of Mr. Simms?"

"It appears that way, but we have no way of knowing for sure," Hudson admitted with a small wince.

Silence descended over the room until Hudson clapped his hands together. "And now for the news that I can't wait to share with you."

Madalene leaned forward in her seat in anticipation.

"Lord Stafford has found a buyer for Mowbray Hall and his Scottish estate," Hudson continued. "After an intense negotiation on your behalf, he has agreed to pay you £30,000."

"£30,000?" A bright smile came to Madalene's face. "How is this possible? I thought you said I would receive hardly anything after his creditors were done with him."

"Apparently, a solicitor contacted him and offered a generous sum to buy both estates and all the furnishings for his client," Hudson explained.

"This person bought everything?" she asked, her smile dimming.

Hudson nodded. "He did. The tapestries, paintings, carpets, furniture…" he listed. "Everything." He gave her a concerned look. "Aren't you happy?"

"Yes, oh yes." She nodded, but she didn't smile.

Hudson arched an eyebrow. "What's wrong?"

"Would it be possible to contact the new owner about buying back some of my family's more sentimental items?" she asked.

"It may take some time. The buyer wished to remain anonymous," Hudson replied.

"Would you mind making some inquiries, please?" she asked, forcing a smile.

Hudson returned her smile. "For you, anything."

"Please, don't worry yourself, Maddie," Everett assured her. Reaching out, he placed his hand over the clenched fist in her lap. "It will all work out, I'm sure."

Madalene glanced at him, and he could see the sadness in her eyes. "I was hoping to buy back the portraits of my mother and father," she admitted. "Sometimes I fear my memory is fading, and I'm forced to close my eyes in order to recall what they even looked like."

Hudson cast him a concerned look before he turned his attention back to Madalene. "With funds at your disposal, what do you intend to do now?"

"I don't know yet," she admitted. "I was thinking I might retire to Benham Manor for the rest of the Season."

"Truly?" Everett shifted in his seat to face her. "You would leave London even after what we've previously discussed?"

"I still believe it would be for the best," she replied, averting her gaze from his.

"How can you even say that?" he asked in confusion.

Glancing over at the duke, she lowered her voice, "First, I wouldn't be relying on the charity of others anymore. I would be the mistress of my own estate."

"But what about us, Maddie?" Everett asked, frowning. "I know you care about me."

"I do, but remember, there was never supposed to be an '*us*'."

Everett briefly acknowledged the sound of booted footsteps before the study door closed. They were finally alone, and he refused to let Madalene leave this room until she consented to be his real fiancée.

He reached into the pocket of his jacket and pulled out the note. He held it up for her examination, and her face paled. In that moment, he knew she meant every word of what she'd written.

Madalene felt the blood drain from her face as Everett held up the note that he was never supposed to see. Mortification washed over her. She considered jumping up and fleeing from the room, but something kept her rooted in her seat.

"How did you get that note?" she asked in a shaky voice.

"It doesn't matter how I got the note." He tucked it back into his pocket. "What matters, is that I've read it, and I have a question."

"What kind of question?" she asked, rising and walking over

to the window. She wanted to create as much distance as possible between them.

He was watching her closely, and his eyes held an intensity that she had never witnessed before.

"Did you mean what you wrote?"

She ducked her chin into her chest to hide her growing blush. What must he think of her?

Rising from his seat, Everett stepped over and placed his finger under her chin, lifting her head up so she would look at him.

"Do you want to know what I think?" he asked gently.

Madalene didn't respond, couldn't respond, but she kept staring at him, becoming mesmerized by the brown flecks in his blue eyes.

"I think you meant every word, but you never intended for me to get the note." He smirked knowingly. "At least, while you were still alive."

Drawing strength from deep within her, she replied, "I did mean every word."

A smile brightened his face. "That pleases me, Maddie." He brought his hand up to cup her right cheek. "Do you want to know why?"

She nodded.

He leaned closer to her ear and whispered, "Because I am in love with you."

She gasped and turned her head towards him, so their faces were only inches apart. "You are?"

Chuckling, he responded, "I don't know when I started falling in love with you, but I suspect it began the moment you fell into my curricle."

Everett brought his other hand up to cup her other cheek, cradling her face in his hands. "I want to turn this engagement into a real one. I want to marry you, and I don't want to wait until the end of the Season."

"When do you want to marry?"

"Tomorrow, and I have taken the liberty of securing a special license," he said, removing his hand and patting his jacket pocket.

Her lips parted in disbelief. "Tomorrow?"

"Don't you love me, Maddie?" he asked earnestly.

"I do… but…"

He cut her off. "And don't you want to be with me?"

"I do…"

Everett pressed his mouth to hers, kissing her softly. He leaned back with a boyish grin. "I believe I've found my favorite way to silence you."

Sliding down onto one knee, he asked, "Lady Madalene Ramsbury, will you do me the great honor of marrying me tomorrow?"

She wanted to shout yes, but she had a few questions of her own. "Why me?"

"Pardon?"

"Why would you pick me over all the other women of the ton?"

"Because all those women aren't *you,*" he said, smiling as he rose.

"Surely someone that doesn't have a tattered reputation would make a better marchioness," she suggested hesitantly.

"Possibly," he responded, shrugging one shoulder.

She was astonished by his answer, but before she could react, he leaned in and kissed her cheek.

"I don't want anyone else, Maddie. I want *you.*" He kissed her other cheek. "You make me laugh." He kissed her forehead. "And, most importantly, I never knew what I was missing from my life until I met you. You have brought joy back into my life."

"I love you, too," she replied, enjoying his lips lingering on her skin.

"I know." He leaned back. "I could see it in your eyes."

Feeling bold now, she leaned forward and brushed her lips against his, then leaned back slightly.

"Did I do that right?"

"You did just fine." He chuckled. "But perhaps we should practice some more."

Leaning forward, he pressed his lips to hers, kissing her deeply, but in no way controlling. She was thrilled that he was allowing her to set the pace. Madalene never wanted this moment to end. She wanted to stay wrapped up in Everett's arms forever and feel the warmth of his lips on hers. In his arms, she felt whole, complete.

"My answer is yes," she whispered against his lips.

"Yes?" he asked as he started trailing kisses down the side of her neck.

She laughed. "I will marry you tomorrow."

"You will?" He brought his gaze back up to meet hers.

"I will," she repeated.

"Are you truly sure?" A mischievous smile spread across his lips.

"Pardon?"

"Perhaps you need more convincing?" He waggled one eyebrow.

Madalene started to giggle, and she did not complain as he silenced her laughter by pressing his lips to hers. Her heart was so full that she thought it might burst with joy. What's more, she decided that kissing was quickly becoming her favorite pastime.

She didn't know how long they kissed, but a knock at the door caused them both to jump apart.

The door opened, and Penelope stuck her head in. "May we come in?"

"No," Everett said in a hoarse voice, causing her to smile.

Nicholas's voice came from behind Penelope. "Remind him that he is in *my* study."

"I will, dear," Penelope remarked as she walked further into the room. Nicholas and Hudson were close behind.

"Well?" Hudson gave his brother an expectant look.

For a moment, Everett grew solemn. Then, he gleefully announced, "She agreed to marry me!"

The room erupted in cheers, and Madalene soon found herself being embraced by Hudson.

"Welcome to the family," he said. "I knew you were Everett's match from the moment I saw you."

"Thank you," she replied, stepping back.

Penelope came up and embraced her. "I am so happy for you. Isn't it a marvelous feeling to be in love?"

"It is." Her eyes traveled over to Everett, and he met her gaze. "It truly is."

Hudson clasped his brother on the shoulder. "Mother wanted me to inform you that she had anticipated this outcome all along, and she's been planning an engagement ball."

"We don't intend to wait that long," Everett said, reaching for her hand. "Madalene has agreed to marry me… tomorrow."

"Tomorrow?" Nicholas asked. "I daresay you should wait until the banns are posted and give Madalene the Season she deserves."

"That's where you're wrong, your grace." Madalene squeezed her fiancé's hand. "Everett has already given me the perfect Season."

"Bah," Nicholas said. "You're blinded by love."

"Is that so bad?" Madalene smiled.

"It will be when Mother hears about you wanting to marry tomorrow," Hudson replied, but there was no judgement in his voice.

"Now that Madalene is in my arms, I have no desire to ever be apart from her again," Everett declared. "She's my love match, in every sense of the word."

Hudson chuckled. "You've turned sappy, Brother."

"Then so be it," Everett replied, shrugging.

As Madalene listened to her friends banter back and forth, she realized that Everett had been right. She had never been truly alone. Her friends had become her family. And Everett… he completed her. Being with him was enough.

EPILOGUE

"Where are we going, husband?" Madalene asked as she sat next to Everett in the swaying coach.

"I've told you countless times, my dear, I'm not going to tell you until we arrive."

"But we have been traveling for hours," she grumbled as she shifted in her seat to face him. "Yet, you still refuse to let me open the drapes."

"Do you want me to entertain you, wife?"

"Yes, please."

He smiled. "What do you have in mind?"

"Do you know any good jokes?"

"No."

"Can you recite any poems?"

He shook his head.

"Will you sing for me?"

"No."

"You are rather a useless husband, then, aren't you?" she teased.

"Useless, am I?" He wrapped his arm around her waist,

tugging her closer. "Perhaps I need to teach you a lesson in usefulness."

"Yes, please," she murmured, her eyes darting to his lips.

Leaning closer, he pressed his lips to hers. He had just deepened the kiss when the coach jerked to a stop.

Madalene laughed when Everett muttered a few curse words under his breath.

"Don't worry, we can pick up where we left off later," she murmured.

"Do you promise?" he asked breathlessly.

She brushed her lips against his. "Always."

The door to the coach opened, and Everett stepped out. He reached back in to assist her. As she stepped down, she froze.

"This is Mowbray Hall!" she exclaimed in disbelief.

Her eyes swept over the sprawling four-level estate. The main entrance was embellished with four turrets, and the window frames were highlighted with gold leaf, which were designed to catch the setting sun.

"Surprise!" Everett announced. "Welcome home."

"I'm afraid I don't understand."

He placed his arm around her shoulder as she continued to gaze at her ancestral home. "I was the anonymous buyer that bought Mowbray Hall and the estate in Scotland."

"You?"

He nodded. "It's my wedding gift to you."

"Oh, Everett!" she cried. "This is too much."

"Does it displease you?" he asked, sounding alarmed.

"Heavens, no." She paused. "It's perfect."

He removed his arm from around her shoulder and extended it towards her. "I have another surprise for you."

"Another one?"

The door to the estate opened, and Mr. Hayward stepped out with a smile on his face.

"Hayward," she greeted him. "It's good to see you looking so well."

"Lord Northampton was gracious enough to hire me away from Lord Stafford, at a substantial pay raise, I might add," Hayward revealed.

Feeling elated, Madalene stood on her tiptoes and kissed her husband. "Thank you, Everett."

"Come, there is something that I wish to show you," he said, leading her inside.

He didn't stop until they reached the parlor. Above the fireplace was the portrait of her mother, dressed in her finery.

Madalene stepped closer, her eyes filling with tears. How she missed her mother!

"Your father's portrait is in the library," Everett said, coming to stand next to her.

"Thank you, husband," she whispered, knowing her words were not enough thanks for such a thoughtful gift.

Reaching into his pocket, Everett pulled out two portrait miniatures and extended them towards her.

"I had an artist create a copy of each portrait, so you can always have them near you."

"Oh, Everett!" Clasping the miniature portraits in her hand, Madalene sighed. "That was most thoughtful of you. I'm so glad that I chose to marry you."

"I must say, I'm relieved, for we have been married for less than a week. If you had tired of me so soon…"

"Six glorious days," she interrupted, stepping closer to him. "And I love you more every day."

The sound of the main door being thrown open, echoed throughout the lower level of the estate. A moment later, Hudson strode into the parlor with a determined look on his face.

"What is wrong?" Everett's face paled. "Did something happen to Mother?"

Hudson shook his head. "No, Mother is fine."

"Then, what's wrong?"

"Lord Stafford is dead." Hudson revealed with a frown.

"Dead?" Madalene repeated.

"Yes. I was just notified by his solicitor, Mr. Cooke, and I came straightaway to inform you."

"How did you know we were at Mowbray Hall?" Everett asked curiously.

"I stopped by your townhouse," Hudson said, walking further into the room. "Mother informed me that you had taken Madalene to see her wedding gift."

Madalene didn't speak for a long moment before she approached the settee and sat down.

"How did he die?" she asked softly.

Hudson frowned as he exchanged a worried look with Everett.

"Last night," he began, looking back at Madalene, "he was at a gambling hall and heated words were exchanged. It appears that he angered the wrong people." He hesitated before adding, "His body was found in the River Thames this morning."

"What a fitting death," Everett muttered under his breath.

Hudson stepped to the mantel and looked up at the portrait. "Your mother was beautiful," he commented.

"Thank you," Madalene murmured.

"Mother wanted me to inquire if it was still all right to proceed with the ball tonight," Hudson asked, turning back towards them.

Everett lifted his expectant brow at her. "What do you say, Maddie? If you'd like to postpone the ball, everyone would understand. You just lost your uncle."

"That's not necessary," she replied. "Your mother has been painstakingly planning this ball for days, and I dare not disappoint her."

"Are you sure?" Everett asked.

"I am." She smiled. "I find that I am quite eager to waltz with my husband tonight."

"Then, I will depart and let Mother know," Hudson said, bowing.

"Thank you," Everett acknowledged.

As Hudson left the room, Everett came and sat down next to her. "How are you faring?"

"Is it sad that I am relieved he's dead?"

"Not at all," Everett reassured her. "I believe he got his just desserts."

"As do I," she replied.

"Your uncle can never hurt you again," he reassured her, slipping his arm around her shoulder.

"For that, I'm grateful." She leaned back against him. "Although, he was still my family, and you can't pick your family."

"True," Everett huffed. "*No one* would willingly pick Stafford to be in their family."

"I am glad that I picked you, husband." She turned in his arms and kissed him on the lips.

"And I'm glad that I suggested that we get engaged in the first place."

"That was a rather clever alliance," Madalene agreed.

The End

COMING SOON:

A Reluctant Guardian: A Regency Romance
Book 2 of Regency Brides: A Promise of Love Series

Coming Soon:

Preorder Now

Baldwin, the Viscount of Mountgarret, was finally content with his life. Unexpectedly, his childhood friend dies, leaving him his most prized treasures: his two young daughters. Baldwin's priorities begin to shift as he arrives home and meets his wards' infuriatingly stubborn governess. His interest is piqued by the mystery surrounding her, but she's only a governess. He certainly can't pursue her. Can he?

After three "unsuccessful" Seasons, Emeline Warren discovers a heinous plot to force her into marriage with an aging earl. She flees from her ancestral home and unwittingly becomes a governess to two little girls. Finding herself attracted to their reluctant guardian, she's determined not to fall prey to his charms.

Can two unlikely lovers let go of their foolish pride, or will they lose what matters most?

ABOUT THE AUTHOR

Laura Beers spent most of her childhood with a nose stuck in a book, dreaming of becoming an author. She attended Brigham Young University, eventually earning a Bachelor of Science degree in Construction Management.

Many years later, and with loving encouragement from her family, Laura decided to start writing again. Besides being a full-time homemaker to her three kids, she loves waterskiing, hiking, and drinking Dr. Pepper. Currently, Laura Beers resides in South Carolina.

You can reach her at authorlaurabeers@gmail.com

Printed in Great Britain
by Amazon

37117366R00136